Noah and the Academy of the Gods:
A Hallucinatory Voyage

By Yair Riback and Nira Riback

Dear Michael and Margie,
Yair and I truely cherished
all the years of friendship
with your parents, appreciating
their caring and devotion.
From Yair that is not here with us
any more.
From me
With love
Nira

CHAPTER 1

I have a recurring dream where I am walking across a flat plain. It seems endless, stretching beyond the horizon. Above me, the sky is bright blue, without a single cloud or bird. There is nothing on this plain; no trees, no hills, no rocks, not even a pebble. No matter what direction I travel in, or how far I walk, nothing changes. It is as if I'm not even moving. If I sit down to rest, I wake up, so I must keep walking in order to remain asleep. I never get tired from walking, but I get weary of the emptiness and the sameness of the unchanging landscape. I tire of the futility of my efforts. There is no hope, no sign of it ending.

The ground is hard, so I can't leave any footprints behind me to trace my path. One night I stopped to mark my place, making a hole in the ground as a reference point. Now, each night the dream occurs I begin at the hole and start walking away from it.

Maybe God also experienced this. He was wandering in the universal void, made heaven and earth to mark his place, and then he wandered away. The earth is his reference point, and he might stumble upon it again one day, but he won't be unable to stay. If he stays, he will wake up, and the earth will disappear and vanish with his sleep.

***

The line of people waiting to enter the King Tut special exhibit at the museum extended for a couple of city blocks. The line was moving at a snail's pace. My only consolation was looking at the people behind me, but it was the crowd of people in front who frustrated me. Every one of them was robbing a chunk of my time, and after finally making it inside, I'd be walking behind them and past the exhibits at their pace, unable to stop where I wanted and for the amount of time I wished. I would be looking over their heads, carried from one place to another by the crowd. Their constant noise and nonsensical chatter would make the visit even less desirable. I wished I could make them all disappear and have the entire exhibit to myself, then I could take all the time I wanted to enjoy the museum. This was where I "met" Pam for the first time. After we were married, we began to refer to this as our first date and invented all the details of how we met at the museum. We both visited the museum that day, but not together, and the probability that we actually passed by each other is actually very low.

Pam was somewhere behind me in the line, and there were dozens of people between us. Had I been with her, the long wait would have been easier. But, at that moment, I had never met her. However, we agreed that as I waited, I was talking to her in my imagination as if she stood in line in front of me.

"Hi. I'm Noah Miller."

"Nice to meet you. I'm Pamela, but you can call me Pam."

I complained that my feet were hurting from the long wait and suggested we leave. Then, I smiled at her, and she smiled back. A few minutes later, I said, "This is taking forever."

"Forever is short for King Tut," she said. I fell in love with her at that moment.

Then I made the first mistake of our relationship. I suggested we leave and go to a movie or somewhere else instead of continuing to wait in line.

"We can go to the movies some other time, but this exhibit won't be here for long," she replied. I noticed she used "we," and now I was ready to stay for as long as it would take. "It's like visiting a time capsule," she added.

In reality, I entered the museum about an hour later, and Pam entered it about half an hour after me.

I remember nothing about the first important event in my life. I was eleven months old when a drunk driver killed my mother. We were driving home from the grocery store. She stopped at a red light, and the drunk driver hit us head-on as my mother leaned over me to tighten the safety belt around my car seat. Her body came between me and the dashboard, and the softness of her body saved my life. For a short instant, we were united in the dark. This is why I have never been afraid of the dark. It feels safe and soft, like her body.

The jolt against my mother's body shook my head, and the pressure created new connections between the two halves of my brain, fusing them together in uncommon patterns, different from other people's brains. Sometimes one side dominates the other, or sometimes they work together in unique ways. The right half is imaginative and creative, while the left half is rational and logical. My radiation sensitivity comes from the right half of my brain. This is something I have kept a secret as an adult, because no one would understand it, let alone believe me. I haven't even shared this with Pam.

When I was younger I tried to describe my radiation sensitivity to other people, but this only resulted in them viewing me as peculiar, maybe crazy. I learned to be strategic about what I revealed so I would be accepted by my peers.

Most people are completely unaware of the radiation around us, but it is everywhere. Nothing stops it. It penetrates matter and goes through human bodies and brains. Gradually, it changes the patterns of human brain waves, and soon everyone will have the same wave pattern.

The world is full of radiation. It was with God prior to the beginning. It saturates the world and is all around us. And I can see it.

When the right half of my brain dominates, I see radiation colors that no one else can see; colors without names, colors that are beyond words. The best way I can explain it is that to me, the color red is like the sound of a trumpet. I don't see the "true" colors of things—Pam is convinced I'm color blind.

In the evening I often see the flickering bluish hues of radiation coming out from television sets in the houses in our neighborhood. The radiation fills up the rooms and spills out of the windows and into the street—the entire city is swelling with the blue hue of radiation. I have seen these rich colors all my life, but recently the right side has become more dominant.

The first time I noticed something really unusual was one morning when, returning from my morning jog, I heard the telephone ringing. By the time I fished out the key from my sweatshirt pocket, unlocked the front door, and reached the phone, it had stopped ringing. The strange thing was that Pam heard nothing.

"What phone?" she asked.

"Ours of course."

"Are you joking? The phone hasn't rung at all this morning."

The ringing was the first sign the right side of my brain was becoming more active, but it took me some time to realize this. At first, I paid no attention to it, but since Pam heard nothing, the ringing should have immediately alerted me that something was happening. I dismissed it with rational explanations, because none of the things that happened after this were by themselves unusual occurrences. It was only their degree and frequency that made them bizarre, and each of them could be rationalized away.

"Take a look at this," Pam said while we were eating breakfast later that morning. She pointed to the front page of the morning paper. The headline read "Termites Threaten the World Atmosphere," and the article opened by describing how "Dr. Gray from Y. University discovered that termites emit more methane gas than all the industrial nations put together . . . the greenhouse effect is imminent . . . Methane gas is a major cause of the ozone layer's depletion."

Farther down, the article continued, "Dr. Gray estimates there are 1,500 pounds of termites for every person." I figured this meant there were more than 5 million hungry mouths for every man, woman, and child; 5 million termites chomping wood and farting out methane gas. I imagined hearing the 5 million mouths that were my share making terrible sounds.

Reading this made me depressed. I felt a pending doom hanging over me and the rest of the world. Nukes or no nukes, war or peace, the sun cooling or warming, overpopulation and world hunger or worldwide population control, finding a cure for cancer or not, the list went on, and no matter what we do, no matter how hard we try, nothing will help. Nothing will save the world as long as the termites keep chomping into the flesh of the wood—into the life of the world.

I saw a ray of light coming in through the window. It landed on the cereal box, like it was trying to draw my attention to it. I picked up the box. The side label listed all the ingredients and their nutritional value, but because of the termites, the flesh will perish no matter what ingredients we consume. What about the spirit? The spirit might be immortal. Suddenly it came to me. The human spirit must be saved. Its major attributes must be preserved. I needed to create a time capsule that could demonstrate human greatness, or at least serve as a warning to whoever finds it so they can avoid our pitfalls. The basic elements of human society must be assembled and kept in a safe place until someone in the future finds it.

The phone rang again. This time Pam heard it and answered. The call was for me.

I'm a food engineer at the Omega Corporation, a large conglomerate whose tentacles latch onto everything, including high-technology electronics and fast-food franchises, and there have been rumors at work that I am going to be promoted to manager of my department.

A secretary was calling to let me know that Mr. Brown, Omega's executive director, wished to see me in person. I got a lump in my throat. The rumors might be true.

"Will two o'clock tomorrow work?" she asked.

I managed to utter a sound, which she interpreted as agreement, not that it really mattered. Mr. Brown was summoning me, anytime was good.

I arrived fifteen minutes early to the appointment the next day. I couldn't keep Mr. Brown waiting.

Omega's headquarters isn't an imposing structure. It has a tinted glass façade, like most of the other office buildings downtown. Pam is an interior designer, and her firm had done work in the building. She had been responsible for the décor in the Omega offices and waiting room. I had visited the space a few times, just to see her handiwork, and I liked the soft colors and airy spaces that were typical of her style.

But something was terribly wrong. The waiting room's décor wasn't Pam's design. I was deeply disappointed by the changes and afraid it was a bad omen. Now there was a tasteless assortment of furniture, each a different style and in mismatched colors; heavily upholstered armchairs beside a light contemporary coffee table, three lamps, each a different style, and the walls covered with geometric red, blue, and yellow wallpaper. Even the good art had vanished, and now there were pictures of people hunting, fishing, and playing golf all over the walls. I made a mental note to remember the details. Pam would love to find out which of her competitors was responsible for this atrocity!

This was not all that was amiss. Sitting behind the desk was a young secretary with empty, glazed eyes. She was chewing gum and blowing bubbles in between answering the phone.

"Do you want a cup of coffee, sir?" she asked as she blew a large bubble that collapsed on her face with a gentle puff.

I could use some coffee but was certain that Mr. Brown would be ready to see me any moment now. I wondered why she was acting in such a strange manner. She retrieved the gum membrane from her face, put it back into her mouth, and blew it into a bubble again.

I thumbed through some old magazines that were laying on the coffee table. I started looking through an outdated women's clothing catalog. It was a little past two now. I got up, pretending to look for more magazines, but I was really trying to draw the secretary's attention. I was getting anxious.

Fifteen minutes later I got up again, this time pretending to examine one of the silly paintings on the wall. I coughed to try to draw the secretary's attention. She didn't look at me. I walked back to the chair where I had been sitting, slowly so as not to admit my defeat.

Twenty minutes later I was finally told Mr. Brown was ready to see me. I hurried through a glass door and found myself in a long corridor. I saw an elevator and what seemed like dozens of baby blue doors. I didn't know where I was supposed to go. The doors had no numbers or names on them. I went around the corridor, looking for a directory of some kind, but I found myself back at the glass door where I had started. It was locked. I waved my hand at the secretary on the other side of the door, trying to draw her attention so she would come and tell me where to go. I drew her attention alright, but she simply waved back at me. For a while, we continued waving at each other. I called out to her from behind the door, but she didn't hear me. Finally, I gave up. I felt helpless, and my heart was beating fast. I started to wander down the corridor. Next to the elevators was a janitor emptying the garbage can.

"Can you tell me where Mr. Brown's office is?" He looked from side to side as if making sure I wasn't talking to someone else.

"Why ask me?"

"There's no one else here." He looked around again, checking to see if this was true.

"Eleventh floor," he said in a hurry and left before I could even thank him.

I waited for an elevator to come. Why would Mr. Brown's office be three floors up? Wouldn't it make more sense for his office to be on the same floor as the waiting room? After a long time, the two elevators came at once, both going down. I pressed the up button. Once again they both came, going down. I kept pressing the button until they came a third time; this time going up. The elevator stopped at each floor on the way up, but no one was waiting.

The doors on the eleventh floor were painted pink, and there weren't any numbers, names, or even a directory on this floor either. My frustration turned into panic. Streams of cold perspiration crawled down my body. I began opening the doors, but all the offices were empty. It was now after three. My panic was growing with every minute. I touched the walls to check if they were real, hoping this was a nightmare and I was dreaming. The walls were solid. I kept walking along the corridors of the eleventh floor until I heard a clicking sound.

I turned a corner and saw a woman pounding away on a large typewriter. I was so delighted to see her I didn't stop to consider how odd it was for her to be using such an antiquated object—in an Omega office no less, which should have the most up-to-date Omega-brand office equipment.

"I'm here to see Mr. Brown. Mr. John Brown," I emphasized every word, "the executive director."

"Oh," she replied, clearly unimpressed.

"Look here, young lady. I have an appointment with Mr. Brown, and I'm late already. Will you please tell me where the hell his office is?"

"No need to swear, sir." She sounded hurt. "It's not my fault you're late." She took a deep breath and continued in a calmer voice, "I'll be glad to help you, but I don't know where his office is."

"Who does know?"

She shrugged her shoulders.

"Can you call and find out?!"

"I suppose so."

I was losing my temper. She picked up the phone, looked at it, then put it back down.

"I can't."

"Why the hell not."

"Security, you know."

"So? Call security and ask."

"They won't give out the information over the phone."

"Can someone come here and show me then?"

"They're too busy; they can't leave their post for every stranger who comes here."

I was so angry, I was ready to tear her apart, but I left before I was tempted to act on these impulses. As I was leaving, I heard her resuming her typing.

The next door I came to was the ladies room. I entered and saw a woman was standing at the mirror doing her makeup.

"Pervert."

"Sorry, ma'am. Can you tell me where . . ."

"You better get lost before I call security."

Next door, in the men's room, a man was washing his hands.

"I'm looking for Mr. Brown's office." I was surprised by my calm voice.

"Mr. John Brown, you mean?" He said as he turned toward me. "You must be new. Let me give you a bit of advice. Here, you know only what you're supposed to know, no more no less. And don't ask questions about what you don't know."

"That's a smart policy. I'll try to remember it, but I have an appointment with Mr. Brown." I informed him.

"I'm afraid I can't help you. You have to know where to go. He who knows doesn't speak, and he who speaks doesn't know."

"Please." I pleaded. I had no time for policy discussions.

"All right, but I'm risking my job." He looked around, whispered "thirteenth floor" into my ear, then left in a hurry. I headed back toward the elevators.

The doors on the thirteenth floor were painted brown. I felt I was making progress: Mr. Brown, brown doors. At the end of the main corridor was a set of large double doors. I pulled them open with both hands and entered.

"Mr. Miller, I'm glad you came." Mr. Brown was sitting at a large desk and behind him was a magnificent view of the river.

"Sit," he said simply.

No word about my tardiness. There was no need for the apology I had prepared.

When I left the office, there were numbers on the doors; they were small, but they were there, as well as a directory. I could have easily missed them because of my anxiety. And the waiting room was decorated the way Pam had designed it.

I now know that the strange events were visions from the right half of my brain. But on that day, I tried to rationalize my peculiar experiences.

The elevators were easy to explain: everyone is frustrated by them, especially when you are in a hurry. The hallways could have been recently repainted, tasteless as they were, and the numbers temporarily removed. There could be two different waiting rooms, the one I has seen on previous visits to the building with Pam and the one I waited in that day, and the secretary could just have had a bad day.

I felt exhausted after the strain of trying to reach Mr. Brown and then meeting with him, so I stopped at a park to relax and enjoy the beautiful weather. As I watched the clouds drift by in the sky, thoughts and memories passed through my mind. There was one memory in particular that I enjoyed returning to and reliving over and over again.

CHAPTER 2

We were heading out on one of our trips. My dad, my stepmom Louise (whom my Dad and I call Lou), my five-year-old half-sister Oedi (I couldn't pronounce Melody when she was born and the nickname stuck), and nine-year-old me were all piled in the car.

As soon as we reached the outskirts of the city, Oedi fell asleep and remained asleep for most of the journey. I didn't mind yielding most of the back seat to her, as long as she was quiet and left me alone so I could enjoy the trip. It wasn't the trip itself I enjoyed so much as the imaginary games we played. Dad came up with different ideas all the time. This made the long hours of driving tolerable. The games were always somehow related to the area we were driving through.

Dad usually did most of the driving, while Lou was the navigator, an unnecessary function this time since we were just traveling to visit the places that happened to appear along the way. We followed signs to places with strange or uncommon names, like "Big Hollow" or "Gravel Junction." When my friends bragged about visiting large cities, I teased them, "Guess where I've been . . . Monkey's Eyebrow." And everyone laughed, not believing me.

"Where are we?" Dad would occasionally ask.

"Here, halfway between this and that," Lou would say, pointing to a random place on the map in her lap.

We started a new game that trip. We were space explorers on a mission to discover new worlds and unknown civilizations. Our mission was to make contact with these civilizations and establish friendly relationships with them. Dad, Captain Miller, was a renowned anthropologist and the head of the expedition, Lou was the chief science officer, and Oedi was a yeoman—I never found out what a yeoman's duties were. I was the junior science and security officer.

"Our life-detecting device is showing no signs of life on this planet," I reported to the captain.

"Are you sure there isn't a malfunction?"

"No, sir, the detector is working fine."

All the roads were empty, and the towns that we passed seemed deserted. There were no signs of life, and although here or there we saw smoke coming from some houses, there were no signs of sentient life in the streets.

However, the planet was rich with oxygen, and its atmosphere was similar to our own. Its rich vegetation indicated that there was plenty of freshwater. The skies were blue, like on our planet, and there were white clouds, which also looked like those on our planet. The fields were green, we saw several irrigation systems sprinkling water, but there were no living creatures to be found.

"Security Officer Noah, activate the cloaking device," ordered Captain Miller.

"Yes, sir." I manipulated the controls that were hidden behind the ashtray. "Cloaking device activated, sir." We were now in stealth mode, invisible and undetectable. It was a standing order of space command that a landing party remain in stealth mode until friendly contact is established.

There were no signs of the aliens who had paved the roads we traveled on, and we didn't see any of their vehicles either. Other signs of a living civilization were also absent. Our radio scanners, for example, received nothing but static noise. On our home planet, the air practically explodes with radio transmissions, and every frequency is loaded with communication signals, music, talk, and every other imaginable sorts of signal, not to mention colorful television broadcasts. This planet was mute. It was lifeless and beautiful, but it did contain signs of lifeforms who had been capable and industrious.

"Maybe the aliens saw us coming and are using cloaking devices of their own," I suggested, but immediately regretted saying so. This theory didn't explain the absence of lower lifeforms.

"Illogical," chief science officer Lou responded.

"Maybe there was a war?" I tried again, although there were no signs of war, no destruction, anywhere.

"What can we learn about this civilization?" asked Captain Miller. That was the game's key question. We were trying to learn about the planet from what its inhabitants had left behind.

"Industrious, no doubt," said the chief science officer.

"They were very advanced. They even had antenna dishes," I offered. Bingo! This time even the skeptical chief science officer agreed with me.

"Very good Officer Noah. These must be some kind of primitive antennas, maybe like those on twentieth-century Earth, or maybe even more primitive than that."

"And what do you make of the symbols on them?"

"Some kind of language?" Correct again. As a junior science officer, it was also my duty to operate the Galactic Language Translator. This was a portable device—resembling a Walkman radio—that could translate any galactic language into plain English. All you had to do was put on the earphones. It could also scan written language and provide English translations.

I scanned the flat sign boards, but the device couldn't translate many words. They didn't seem to have English equivalents. Words like Texaco, McDonald's, and Holiday Inn must have been meaningful to the local culture. Their frequent repetition pointed to their importance, but the device couldn't translate their message into anything familiar.

In addition to language symbols, the boards also provided pictorial information. We assumed they were the aliens' images, but we found it odd that the locals would portray themselves on the sides of the roads in such a manner. It was now the chief science officer's turn to make an illogical assumption.

"Maybe they're deities of some kind."

Captain Miller ordered me to take pictures so we could study them later.

"Five miles to McDonald's," I said, the Galactic Language Translator's headphones covering my ears. Now we could find out what McDonald's was. We were watching the odometer eagerly, but then Oedi spoiled the magic of the moment. She woke up and stated she had to go pee. Not again, we had stopped half an hour ago, but neither the captain nor the first science officer could refuse her demand. We stopped at a place the Galactic Language Translator said was "Mount Lebanon." Another ghost town.

"Officer Noah," ordered Captain Miller, "you stay behind and be ready to activate the cloaking device at the first sign of trouble. Don't worry if we have problems. You must save the vehicle first."

Captain Miller was following space command's standing orders. I had to stay aboard until it was clear that there was no danger. Captain Miller always acted by the book. Once he was able to confirm that it was safe, I was allowed to leave the shuttle and join the rest of the expedition.

I took a deep breath of the planet's atmosphere. It felt like the air on our planet, but it was better. It had no pollutants and was cool and crisp. I felt intoxicated by it.

We decided to take this opportunity to acquire supplies and fuel and make some initial ground explorations. We discovered they had many machines that dispensed all sorts of objects. We also discovered that using various shapes of Universal Master Decoders—including a plastic card with a magnetic strip capable of breaking any code, paper rectangles that could take on a variety of pictures and numbers to pass as local currency, and different-sized metal coins that could also take on the appearance of local currency—we could use all these machines. Only captains and senior officers were issued decoders.

One of the machines dispensed brightly colored plastic hands. Each one was mounted on a spring and had a suction cup on the bottom so it could be attached to the rear window or dashboard and wave to fellow travelers. Captain Miller handed me a round decoder to use, and I got a green one.

Oedi was hungry now, so we stopped at what appeared to be a local restaurant. Captain Miller talked to a microphone hidden in the wall and ordered hamburgers, fries, and drinks.

"Ten twenty-five," said a voice. There was no one inside, the exchange was between us and an automated electronic device installed in the wall. Captain Miller deposited a few decoders in a receptacle under a tinted-glass window, a mechanical arm scooped up the decoders and then out came our order.

***

The park bench was starting to feel uncomfortable, and this forced my mind back to the present. I saw a few clouds drift by that looked like hands. They were waving at me. I remembered that I had kept the green toy hand from that trip; it was in a box full of childhood mementos that were stored in the attic.

This would be the first item in my time capsule.

CHAPTER 3

"Never been to New York!" There had been disbelief in Mr. Brown's voice. By the time our meeting ended I had been promoted to head of my department, assigned to represent Omega at negotiations with a potential subsidiary company in New York City, and given three extra vacation days to stay and explore the city.

Mr. Brown's secretary booked me a room on the forty-seventh floor of the hotel. I had a panoramic view of the city. Small specks of matter no larger than ants were creeping along below me. The distance filtered away the city's less appealing aspects: no street noise and everything looked clean.

The business negotiations were successfully completed, and now I had three days to be a tourist. I was ready to take a bite from the Big Apple. But, the right half of my brain began to take over.

I decided to start with the first thing on my list, the Metropolitan Museum of Arts. I headed down to the hotel lobby to get directions. Should I hail a cab or attempt to navigate the subway?

The desk clerk didn't see me. He was staring at the far corners of the lobby. His phone rang, and he glanced up at me while taking the call.

"Excuse me, sir," I said when he put the phone down. I was as polite as possible when I asked for directions.

"You want to go to the Met? There are a lot of transfers if you take the subway. You are better off taking a taxi."

I didn't take his advice and took the subway.

I was rocking with the train, like in prayer, with the monotonic sound of the metal wheels on the rails providing devotional music. I sat at the back of the car so I could watch the other passengers. I smiled at a woman who was sitting across from me. She turned her head away nervously and moved to a different seat at the other end of the car.

The sounds of the train and its rhythmic motion had a hypnotic effect, rocking me, making me drowsy, and then jolting me awake. It was not relaxing. Click . . . click . . . click went the train. I was riding among strangers I would never see again. I could be dead, and they wouldn't know or care . . . going about their business . . . they could all be dead, and I wouldn't know . . . all disappear . . .

wouldn't affect me a bit . . . click . . . click . . . click . . . stranger among strangers . . . parallel lines . . .

The dark walls of the tunnel were rushing backward, and they were dotted with tiny rows of lights that were combining into endless strings. I was rocking back and forth as if in ecstasy. The metal wheels kept clicking rhythmically, and the sounds, the darkness, the lights, and the motion all mixed together. I also saw colorful radiation creating an enthralling atmosphere. This wasn't magic, and I wasn't sleeping.

Humans are weak . . . unworthy, only human culture is worthy . . . Humans corrupt culture . . . destroy it . . . wars . . . pollution . . . nuke it . . . my time capsule will save human culture . . . culture exists by its own right . . . it's eternal . . . humans are temporal . . . clicking along . . . clicking away . . . click . . . click . . . click . . .

Suddenly I was alone, and then everything went black.

It was dark in the train station when I regained consciousness. I was in the lowest part of the station, several levels underground. Heavy pillars supported the roof, casting dark shadows that reached the darkest edges of the station and provided a good hiding place for potential assailants. I was alone and apprehensive about the potential danger that lingered there; the lights were too weak and faint to disperse the gloom.

The tracks converged into two black openings on opposite sides. Near one opening was a staircase leading to the upper levels. An express train emerged from one black hole and disappeared in the other.

No more trains came.

The smell of rotting garbage was everywhere. I was pacing around, and it sounded like walking on a coat of wet paint. I glanced at the time and noticed that the station's clocks were frozen. I looked at the two tunnel openings, but I didn't hear the sound of approaching trains, even the vibrations from the upper levels had stopped.

I regretted not listening to the advice of the hotel clerk. I should have taken a taxi.

On the first landing on my way up there was an elderly woman who was lying on the ground and unconscious. Her face revealed no fear, no panic, not even surprise. She was holding a grocery bag in her left hand, its contents were scattered all around her, and her purse lay beside her right hand.

I was taken aback by this discovery. There was no one near her. I was sure the sound of my approach had scared her attacker away. I approached to assist her and help her collect her groceries.

I didn't hear her breathing. My heart began pounding. What should I do? Should I run for help? Should I call the police? I decided to try to find help and headed toward the exit. This was when I noticed something even more horrible. There was a deep silence. The constant murmur of the city, the sound of life, was gone.

I reached the exit and froze in my steps, unable to move for a long time. In horror and disbelief, I saw dozens of people scattered all over the place—on the ground, on benches, leaning against the walls—and none of them were moving or breathing. None of them were alive!

I stood there for a long time, unable to move. What had once been a crowd of people was now a huddle of corpses. Whatever had struck them was sudden and instantaneous.

This silence had swallowed the sounds of the city's life—cars' humming motors, appliances, and screaming sirens—the sounds of the combined commotion of life. This was the terrible silence of a heart that had stopped. It was the sound of death.

Horrible as they were, the sights at the station were only a prelude. The disaster had spared no one.

"Hello? Is anyone alive?" My voice was absorbed by the silence and didn't echo back. There was no answer, so I shouted again and again.

Everything was spinning around me as I walked into the street. I couldn't see clearly.

"Excuse me, I'm sorry," I apologized as I stumbled over on a corpse in my way.

There were bodies on the pavement, at street crossings, in cars, and at bus stops. People had fallen on the spot in the middle of their daily activities: crossing the street, buying newspapers from a smiling corner vendor, or holding hands. Whatever struck was so sudden, they didn't have time to react. I saw no pain in their frozen expressions. The only horror that existed was mine, for I had lived and was spared their horrible fate.

It was the same city, the same buildings, the same streets, and the same trees, only the people had changed. Their life had been snatched away, like a giant appliance cut off from its power source.

Just like the last dinosaur, I was alone.

Maybe this was the wrath of an angry god who had wiped the slate of the world clean to start over again? Or was the right half of my brain playing tricks on me, jolting me from the world of the real into the realm of illusion and nightmare, where I am dreaming the collective nightmare of humanity? But everything I touched was hard and had substance.

I felt desperate and lost. In the back of my mind, I kept hoping that, despite everything, I'd soon wake up, the nightmare would be over, and everything would return to normal again. I had to keep reminding myself that I wasn't sleeping.

"Hello? Is anyone there?" I shouted.

No one answered.

The world had ended, not with a bang but with a whisper. There were no dramatic effects, no spectacular atomic mushroom clouds, no firestorms, no roars of explosions, no destruction, and no instant disintegration of bodies. Perhaps somewhere in space, a device had exploded? It could have been an act of war or an accident. The cause didn't really matter; the end results were the same.

I began running aimlessly down the street.

"Let this nightmare be over. Let it be a nightmare," I repeated to myself.

I stopped at a street crossing and waited for the light to change. Then I realized how ridiculous it was and ran into the middle of the road, laughing hysterically, daring the world to run me over, challenging the world and expecting—no hoping—to be awakened from this madness and arrested for disturbing the traffic. If indeed this was in my head—perceptions associated with the right half of my brain—there was another world out there. If this madness was in me, then out there in the world, cars would be running as usual, and a police officer would soon come to take me away. Nothing of the kind happened.

A paralyzing terror overtook me, but I couldn't scream. The more horrors I saw, the more debilitated I became, and I almost collapsed. Thoughts of Pam and my family were the only things that sustained me. I must find out if this was universal or if it only hit New York. I couldn't bear the idea of them laying on the ground like the people around me.

I entered a small corner restaurant. Greasy meat patties were burning on the grill, and five customers were slumped in various positions at the counter. There was a phone next to the cash register; it was working. I dialed home but only heard the busy signal. I called Pam's office, then my dad and stepmom's house, but I only got more busy signals. Determined to find others who were still alive, I began dialing local numbers from the telephone directory that I found under the counter by the cash register.

"Hello pilgrim," said Jerry Adams, "just because you reached my voice mail doesn't mean you shouldn't leave a message." I left the restaurant number, just in case.

"Seth Smith," said another, "you piss me off man, calling when I'm not available. Leave your message and buzz off." Again, I left the restaurant number. Soon, I stopped leaving messages; finally, I gave up, frustrated by the futility of my efforts. I didn't know what to do next.

My time capsule, which had seemed so urgent just a few days ago, was no longer important. The immortal human spirit I had intended to preserve had perished.

I went back into the street, overwhelmed by the extent of the catastrophe. I felt an emptiness and void growing inside me. Any emotion I might be feeling seemed too banal and meaningless. It was all inadequate when confronted by an event of such cosmic dimensions—it amplified my human insignificance.

I sensed something all around me. I perceived it with my entire being. It was in the ground, in the empty buildings, in the deserted cars, in the trees, and even in the dead people. It was a unifying emotion that combined everything into one entity, planet Earth. It was a transcendent feeling of great relief. It was worldwide, sad jubilation, like a body that has just overcome a serious distress. The world was cured of the human disease that had caused its maladies. I was the last of the human bacteria.

I sat down and cried.

I don't know how long I sat there. Five minutes? An hour? It felt like an eternity. But I eventually pulled myself together, wiped my eyes, and decided to walk toward my original destination, the Met. The late afternoon sun cast long shadows from the building's tall columns. I didn't see any bodies on the stairs or on the landing in front of the museum entrance. It looked like an island of tranquility in the midst of chaos; peaceful and serene, this place seemed like it hadn't been touched by the disaster. The fountain in front of the museum obscured the street, and so, like taking refuge at an altar, I moved to stand behind it. It was as if I crossed an invisible border that separated this place from the rest of the city, and for the first time since I left the subway station, I was not among corpses. This place was empty.

I wanted to rest for a little while. I stood in the cool shade of the fountain, and for an instant, the terrible events of the past few hours didn't seem real. The building's heavy bronze doors swung wide open, inviting me in, and compelled me to enter.

It was empty. Earlier in the day, I had planned to come here so I could observe the best of human culture, but this was no longer important. The dead people outside made it all meaningless. The museum held many artifacts, but the entire city was now one giant artifact—a gigantic time capsule. Only a few hours ago I was hoping this place wouldn't be too crowded. It was deserted, but not in the way I had hoped.

"Hello, is anyone here?" My shout didn't echo. I felt strange because I was committing a sacrilegious act, like shouting in a public library full of readers, but there were no people or guards to reproach me.

A large crystal chandelier lit the large foyer. In the corners were statues representing different human cultures, a marble statue of Venus, the Roman goddess of love and beauty, an African idol, a Northern American totem pole, and the Indian god Shiva, who was dancing and waving his four arms. In the center of the foyer was a pile of twisted metal—contemporary art.

Something compelled me to go further inside. To my right were two sphinxes guarding the entrance to the Egyptian gallery. Their faces were wrinkled from the passage of time, and their granite bodies were crumbling. I could still turn back and leave. But the prospect of once more wandering among the dead was unappealing. The air here was cool. My heart was pounding, and I heard each of its beats. There was a large mural of Osiris sitting in judgment, weighing the souls of the departed, and Anubis delivering the judged to their fate. The guilty are condemned to cross a narrow bridge, and if they stumble and lose their balance they will fall into an abyss of fire.

Ancient artifacts had lost their luster and lay in their cabinets looking dull, without vitality. There were no guards to prevent me from touching them or picking them up, but I didn't do this. There was no meaning to it; no more excitement associated with illicit actions.

This place had been touched by the disaster after all. The substance of the exhibits had changed. They were no longer samples of human genius, representing various cultures, but a meaningless collection of dead objects. Their luster was drawn from the living who flocked to see them. They were intimately bound together. The living projected their vital energy into the artifacts, and there wasn't enough energy in me alone to project vitality into them.

I entered a different gallery. The Greek and Roman gods had aged without dignity. Their marble faces no longer smiled with serene wisdom; they were now full of loathing and disgust. I stood in front of Mars, the god of war, who was middle-aged, balding, had a large beer belly, and was leaning heavily on a cane. Venus's breasts were sagging, and there was a malicious smile on her wrinkled face.

In another gallery Shiva, prince of dancers, was frozen mid-stride. His cosmic dance had been interrupted. His left foot was lifted in the air, a flame was burning in his palm, and his arm that gestured "don't be afraid" was broken.

I wandered along the museum halls, as I had wandered in the streets, aimlessly, like in a dream, not completely cognizant of what was around me. I didn't pay much attention to the exhibits. As I was doing this I started hearing a steady ticking sound coming from somewhere inside the museum, like from a distant clock.

I eventually wandered into the dimly lit contemporary galleries. I was surrounded by abominations of nature, demons, and twisted bodies; the brain children of distorted minds. There were scattered parts of human bodies. It looked like they had been torn apart by an explosion and their blood splashed on the canvas. Limbs were growing out of random places on the body, never in their normal place, like pieces of a jigsaw puzzle that were put together all in the wrong places. There were eyes staring at me from some paintings; eyes floating in the air, eyes watching me from women's breasts, eyes growing on trees, and Cyclopean eyes pinned on the walls. Some creatures seemed like they had been run through a shredder; others were flat, like they had been run over by a steam roller. There were also cubic people, looking as if they had been compressed into bundles by a car crusher, and clocks were hanging from trees or spread across a dirty picnic table where giant insects were feasting on garbage.

The ticking I was hearing must be coming from a source of radiation inside the museum, and it was growing stronger. I was certain I was not imagining it. It sounded like a giant grandfather clock. It was calling me to it, and I was compelled to find it. I didn't know what it was, but somehow I felt it had to do with the day's events.

When I turned down certain museum halls it was stronger, other times weaker, like in the children's game, giving me hot or cold clues as I approached or turned away from it. It was coming from the medieval section, somewhere among the knights mounted on wooded horses and clothed in iron armor. Their heavy spears were broken, and their swords were dull. They were defeated and broken, at the end of their quest. Here, displayed in a glass cabinet, was the source: a burnished bronze cup surrounded by a bright halo of many colors—the Holy Grail.

I looked at it in awe, mesmerized by its radiant glow. I saw the energy field around it, heard the sound of its radiation, and bathed in its light. Despite everything that had happened, I felt I needed it. If I possessed it, the time capsule would have meaning beyond my original, modest intentions. Moments ago I had abandoned the idea of the time capsule, but now that I had found the Holy Grail it seemed more important than ever.

Using a medieval battle-ax, I broke the glass cabinet and reached for it. I expected my hand to grasp at empty space, like an illusion created by a hologram, but the Holy Grail wasn't an illusion. It was too hot to touch, and my hand recoiled back. I tore off a piece of a knight's gambeson from the exhibit next to it and wrapped the cloth around the cup. Maybe I was deserving, like Sir Galahad, the only knight of the round table who could touch it. I held it close to my body and could feel its heat.

Breaking the glass set off an alarm; the sound of sirens filled the museum. Although no guards were coming, I began running toward the exit. Red arrows pointed the way. I ran fast, not paying attention to any of the exhibits, knocking down display cabinets, and setting off more alarms. The Holy Grail was very hot, but I held firmly onto it, my knuckles turning white from the strength of my grip. When I exited the building, the Holy Grail suddenly cooled off. Its radiation ceased. It was an ordinary cup.

In the street, everything was back to normal. I was shocked once again, but this time by the sights of city life—it was like witnessing another illusion. Cars were running, people were walking in the street, and children were climbing the steps to the museum.

I was afraid that if someone saw the Holy Grail in my possession, I would be in serious trouble. From a distance, I heard the sirens of approaching police cars, but no one was paying attention to me. I hide the cup under my jacket and hailed a taxi. Strangely, the first one stopped. It pulled away just as the police cars arrived, and I could see their lights flashing in front of the museum as we drove away.

It was late in the day when I returned to the hotel. I called Pam right away.

"Are you alright?"

"Of course."

"Are you sure? Did anything unusual happen today?" She was puzzled, and rather than attempt to explain everything to her, I abruptly cut the call short.

I was awake most of the night, gazing at the Holy Grail on the table next to my bed, but it remained cool, emitting no radiation. I was afraid to fall asleep because I might return to the nightmare from earlier. While awake, I was holding onto the present, the normal and rational world; however, I was tired and finally succumbed to a dreamless sleep.

In the morning, I looked through my hotel room window. Everything in the streets below was normal—cars were running and people walking. The city and its people were alive, and the Holy Grail was still on the table. It was not an illusion. I wrapped it in some shirts and hid it under the bed, then I left a Do Not Disturb sign on the door of my room and hurried to return to the Met. I asked the doorman to call me a taxi this time.

"It will be a miracle if you get one at this time of the day. You better take the subway." After yesterday, I believed in miracles.

Several police cars were parked in front of the museum. I climbed the steps slowly, trying to appear as casual as I could and not draw attention. I felt like a criminal returning to the scene of his crime, but I was determined to find answers.

"Good morning, sir," said a policewoman at the entrance. I was startled, caught off guard by such an uncommon gesture. She was beating the palm of her hand with a club.

"Good morning," I answered, not asking what was going on.

At the entrance was a museum gift shop poster advertising a fifty percent discount on a replica of the Holy Grail. I didn't go into the galleries—I was afraid my behavior would give me away—and went into the gift shop instead. On the shelf were several replicas of the Holy Grail.

"It's a nice cup," said the unsmiling sales girl.

"Yes." I tried to remain aloof and indifferent.

"After yesterday's robbery, we should sell them at the regular price," she said.

"Robbery?" My heart began pounding.

"Didn't you see the paper? Someone broke in yesterday and stole the original cup."

"You don't say, it must be worth a fortune."

"No more than this one," she said and smiled. "The original is priceless, but they only display a replica. The original is kept in a vault in the basement."

"So, what's the big deal then?"

"They wouldn't admit it because it could damage their reputation."

I bought one of the replicas. What nonsense this was. How could a mere replica radiate energy?

Back in my hotel room, I put the two next to each other, I couldn't tell the difference. But this really didn't matter. Replica or not, I knew what I saw.

CHAPTER 4

The New York Times that was dropped off outside my hotel room door mentioned the great museum robbery. I expected every policeman to be out looking for me. Every person I passed could be an undercover agent. But they didn't have my picture, and if I played it cool, I could get out of the city without raising suspicion. According to the paper, there was no camera footage from the robbery, but that could be an FBI ploy.

I was confused by yesterday's events. What I first considered a delusion coming from the right half of my brain had materialized in the Holy Grail. I decided to cut my trip short and pretended to be sick so I could get an earlier flight; I was too jittery. I wrapped the Holy Grail in two shirts, placed it inside the gift shop bag with the receipt from when I bought the replica and put it in my briefcase. I tossed the replica down the hotel garbage chute on my way to the lobby.

At the checkout desk, there was a man dressed in plain clothes. He didn't seem to be checking out but stood there looking around. I waited a long time, hiding in the lobby until he finally left. The search seemed to be more intense at the airport. There was a man right behind me, also dressed in plain clothes, and another one pacing back and forth not too far away. I couldn't leave the line without raising their suspicions, so I tried to act as casual as I could, afraid that any nervous movement would give me away. There were also two uniformed police officers standing a short distance from us. I put my briefcase on the floor next to me, just to show how unimportant it was—but it was still touching my foot.

After boarding the plane, I almost jumped out of my seat when a flight attendant touched my shoulder.

"I'm sorry, sir, but all carry-on luggage must be kept under the seat."

I had been holding the briefcase on my lap, and so I proceeded to put it under the seat in such a way that my feet could still touch it. I was fortunate to have a window seat and didn't have to constantly get up to let people through. From time to time I leaned over to look at the briefcase and touch it with my hand. The presence of the Holy Grail gave me a sense of security. I knew it protected me and that nothing bad could happen to me or the plane, but I began to doubt my entire experience in the city. It could have all been a dream. I felt a sudden need to settle my doubts and confirm that the Holy Grail was really there. I got up and brought the briefcase with me to the restroom, half hoping the briefcase would be empty. There it was, just like I had packed it that morning.

The flight attendant's name was Peggy, a name that still fills me with pleasant memories. Peggy was my first love and connected to my early awareness of my radiation sensitivity. I started to daydream about Peggy, our teacher Miss Peel, and our science project.

***

Miss Peel was my seventh-grade science teacher. Every year she taught the same material. She was like an actor playing a role, repeating the same performance over and over again. The performance dictated that I sit behind Peggy in class.

At first, I resented this because I wanted to sit behind Dan, who was my best friend, but it was Miss Peel who made the seating assignments.

"Why can't we sit where we want to, like in Mr. Jones's class?" I dared to ask. It was my first class with her, and I was off to a bad start.

"Because this is my class and not Mr. Jones's. There will be no disorder in my class."

I didn't see the logic of such an answer, maybe it was because everything in science must be predictable and orderly. Order or not, she made me sit behind a girl who always wore her long brown hair in braids. This was Peggy.

I took my disappointment out on her, even though the sitting arrangements weren't her fault. Her long braids annoyed me. They were constantly brushing up against my desk, and they were a good target for revenge. I pinned them to the desk with thumbtacks. Peggy yelled in pain when she tried to get up. I saw Peggy shed a tear, and I immediately regretted what I had done. This was when I realized I liked Peggy.

Miss Peel said she'd pray for me and sent me to the principal's office. When the ordeal was over, Peggy was waiting for me in the hall. We both stood there with our heads down, examining our shoes and not knowing what to say. I snuck a look at her just in time to see her turning her head away. That was when I really fell for her.

"I'm sorry," I said.

"Let's be friends," she replied.

We didn't speak for a couple of days after that, but there was a growing bond between us. Her braids no longer bother me.

Sometimes we stood next to each other in the cafeteria lunch line, but even then we hardly spoke, and we definitely didn't sit together to eat.

Miss Peel managed to make science the most boring subject, making us memorize definitions, facts, and numbers, and I almost gave up on it. My attitude changed the day she came to class and wrote the word radiation, along with other words none of us had heard before, on the chalkboard.

I told Peggy that if there was an atomic fallout, everyone would learn about radiation in a hurry. Somehow Peggy didn't find this amusing.

For reasons I only now understand, I was infatuated with this unit. The first time I associated a clicking sound with radiation was when Miss Peel brought a Geiger counter to class. Until then, I didn't know these were the sounds I was hearing every day. I thought they were my heart beats. I thought the reason why I saw Peggy covered in bright lights was because I liked her. Now I know it was all caused by radiation. When she put the counter next to Peggy, it began clicking like crazy. She was the hottest spot in class.

"Radiation is all around us. Isn't it wonderful?" If Miss Peel thought radiation was so wonderful, she must be like me, able to see its wonderful colors.

When I tried to describe my radiation sensitivity and the wonderful colors to Peggy, she didn't understand.

"If you imagine red as a trumpet and blue as a clarinet, some colors are soft like the harp, others harsh like cymbals . . ." I went on assigning colors to different musical instruments and sounds, but none of this made any sense to her. "To me, colors are like seeing an orchestra of many instruments. Every single color is like a different part of a symphony." At least she didn't make fun of me. She said nothing.

Miss Peel invited the principal to watch the class perform a nuclear emergency drill. We practiced the procedure until we were trained to respond without panic or fear, and when the principal came, she called on the best students to answer her questions. Then, we demonstrated the emergency procedures we had practiced—what to do in case of a nuclear attack, an atomic reactor accident, or a terrorist attack.

We followed the procedures outlined in a government manual. It used cartoons to illustrate what we were supposed to do. The cartoon characters remained calm during the entire ordeal, knowing that if they did the right thing, no harm could befall them, unless they happen to be at ground zero, but the pamphlet assured us that this was a negligible probability.

Miss Peel blew her whistle, and the nuclear emergency drill began. We ducked under the desks and put big brown shopping bags over our heads. We had prepared them ahead of time. The pamphlet didn't say what the probability of always having an empty shopping bag handy was. The bags had no holes in them, and for the duration of the drill, we saw nothing. For some reason, Peggy was trembling, and I held her hand to comfort her. This was the true advantage of the bags. No one could see us holding hands.

The principal asked how we would know when it was safe to come out and remove the bags. Only Randy knew.

"When Squeaky is no longer dead and squeaks again," he said.

Squeaky was a parakeet and the class pet, and Squeaky didn't have a brown bag to protect him. Even the principal allowed one of her rare smiles. But Randy remained serious.

"My father says that one day all the dead will live again, even parakeets," he continued.

The class period ended before we could learn when it was safe to come out; even the manual said nothing about that.

A few days later, Miss Peel assigned us to work in pairs for our projects for the science fair. I asked to work with Dan, knowing she would assign me to work with someone else, most probably with Peggy. It worked.

I spent most of my savings on things for the project. I didn't mind, because it was a way Peggy and I could spend time together, for purely scientific purposes of course. We hardly talked about anything else.

On the day of the science fair, I was surprised to see so many people in the school auditorium, but most of them did have a personal interest, not so much in the exhibits as in the exhibitors.

I was backstage with the others. We were all waiting to present our projects. Although I was sure of winning first place, I was still nervous. From time to time I peeked at the crowd through the curtain. I couldn't see where Lou, my father, and Oedi were sitting, but I knew they were there. I don't remember any of the other projects, but I remember our project was last. Miss Peel said it was a special honor to close the evening, and it really was the climax of the entire show.

The lights were turned off as our project was brought on stage, and when its cover was removed, I heard people gasp. In the center of the stage was a plastic replica of a human body, and different parts were glowing with radiation. I could only imagine how strong the reaction would have been if we had used an anatomically correct model, with its private parts intact. I wanted to use a female mannequin—her breasts glowing in the dark would have been spectacular indeed, like two car headlights. Peggy also thought it was a neat idea, but Miss Peel ruled it out. The only replica Miss Peel approved of was a genderless mannequin, like the people pictured in our biology textbook.

The skeleton of the mannequin was glowing through its plastic skin. The audience saw it as pale yellow—I saw many more colors. This is where strontium would accumulate if a person is exposed to radiation fallout.

Iodine created a purple halo around the mannequin's head. It was shining from its brain, highlighting the intricate brain structure and its blood veins. In the dark, it looked like an angel. Iodine is troublesome stuff when a person is exposed to it. It penetrates the brain through the skin and bloodstream.

We inserted plutonium generously into those organs where it would naturally accumulate after a fallout. They presented an orchestra of colors to my eyes.

Peggy and I shared the presentation and spoke in turns.

"Plutonium-239," I said.

"Plenty in the air around us," said Peggy, making a circle in the air to demonstrate this.

". . . produced by nuclear reactors and nuclear tests . . ."

". . . accumulated in the lungs . . ." I said, pointing at the mannequin's glowing lungs.

". . . and also in the skin . . ." Peggy pointed at its skin, which had a light-green hue to it, like electrons on a computer screen.

The climax of the evening was when the judges announced unanimously that the first prize was awarded to our project. Everyone approved the judges' decision.

Years later, I told Pam about the science fair and Peggy, but she didn't believe it had really happened.

After the fair, Peggy didn't come back to school. I tried calling her home, but the number was disconnected. Peggy had been complaining about headaches and other discomfort, but I hadn't paid attention to this.

A week later, there were rumors circulating that Peggy was not coming back and that she had become an experimental girl. I thought that maybe Peggy got the idea of becoming an experimental girl from our science project. She had been curious about the scientific research into cures for certain illnesses associated with radiation. I rode my bike to Three Mile Lane where she lived, but there was high metal fencing all around it and radiation warning signs. The guard told me that no one was permitted near the house.

"Radon gas from an old nuclear dump site contaminated the entire area. The old drums are leaking, such things happen, you know," the guard told me and shrugged his shoulders.

A few days later, there was an article in the paper about Peggy. Her picture was on the front page under the headline "Girl Headed for Treatment." Miss Peel read the article in class and told us about all the wonderful new organs they'd fit Peggy with.

"One day in the near future, everyone will be able to get these organs. They are immune to disease and injury and are a tremendous improvement on nature. It's like wearing armor. And all this," Miss Peel wiped away a tear, "is thanks to brave people like our dear Peggy. I only hope that humanity will have enough time to accomplish all these wonderful things. Time," she said, "is the only thing humanity can't control. And time is running out." I didn't understand what she meant by this.

"Peggy's artificial blood will not be susceptible to any disease," Miss Peel continued, trying hard to conceal her enthusiasm. "The blood can be mass-produced and save lives in the case of war or other disasters. Her new mechanical heart will never stop, provided its batteries are charged. It will keep beating even after she is dead. The new organs come with eternal warranties." I never saw Miss Peel so emotional.

The only thing they didn't replace was Peggy's brain, but that, according to Miss Peel, changed by itself, and the shape of her brain waves were now flat, like those of the universal energy field.

The following day a television crew from a national network came to our class to make a news segment about Peggy. They spent over an hour interviewing Miss Peel and me, asking questions about the science project, taking pictures of me with the mannequin, and filming me pointing at different features on it. The thrill of appearing on national television made me nervous, and I forgot some of the information; however, the cameraman assured me that after editing I'd be alright. To my great disappointment, they cut the segment down to ten seconds and only showed me sitting behind Peggy's empty desk.

***

A hand touched my shoulder.

"We've landed, sir," said Peggy, the flight attendant.

CHAPTER 5

A surge of radiation had come from my briefcase just before I fell asleep on the plane. No one, not even the person sitting next to me, mentioned anything, but I felt the briefcase burning my feet. Therefore, I don't think I was really asleep: I was catapulted back in time to Miss Peel's class and Peggy. It must have been the Holy Grail causing this and activating the right side of my brain.

By the time we landed, the radiation had stopped and the Holy Grail had cooled. I was certain that when we landed I would be back in my regular environment. However, I wasn't sure when there would be another surge, or what its results would be. I had to be prepared because this could happen at any instant. There was never any warning or indication of when or what the change might be. I was afraid that one time it might be permanent, leaving me trapped where the radiation transported me.

The Holy Grail was unpredictable. It introduced a new element of uncertainty into my world. Maybe there are several different worlds that exist together, side by side, parallel and not touching, and the Holy Grail moves me between them.

Does the Holy Grail truly act at random, or does it reflect some celestial will? There were more questions than answers.

***

I was overjoyed when I spotted Pam at the airport. After the events in the city, riding home in the car with her and seeing the familiar streets and houses gave me a sense of security; reaffirming that this was where I truly belonged. I relaxed. For better or worse, this was my world.

Pam was in a good mood, until I told her about my experiences in the city—all of them. I knew she didn't believe any of it.

"Why not tell me what you really did?"

I insisted on my story, fantastic as it was. I told her about the dead people, my desperate searches, and the phone calls. I could understand her skepticism, so I showed her the cup.

"This is the Holy Grail that I took from the Met. It was emitting radiation when I got it. And the radiation is responsible for everything that happened."

"I don't believe a word of it," she said and picked up the phone to dial the New York police department and confirm if there was a robbery.

"Yes ma'am, there was a robbery . . ." She hung up the phone.

"I still don't believe you did it."

"I told you. There was no one left alive in the entire city. I was sure the world had come to an end."

But she didn't relate my experiences to the end of the world. Without another word, she picked up the phone and called Nancy, the psychotherapist we both were seeing. We had been going to her since before we got married. Pam set up an appointment for me first thing in the morning. I heard her using words such as "emergency" and "hallucinations," which convinced Nancy to make time for me on such short notice.

That night our bedroom was filled with soft blue radiation. Pam didn't see it. It was beyond the spectrum of her vision.

***

Psychologists are like archaeologists of the mind, digging into the past and trying to understand the present. Over the next few weeks, Nancy tried to connect my experience in New York City to the loss of my mother, no matter how much I tried to convince her the events weren't connected. The only thing connected to my mother's death was my radiation sensitivity.

"Why not take a break and take some time to sort things out?" In addition to her private practice, Nancy worked at Our Lady of Mercy. I knew nothing about the place except that it was an institution for people with mental health issues. "Dr. Green is the institution's medical director and an authority on conditions like yours," Nancy said, trying to persuade me to commit myself voluntarily, rather than being committed.

"What's the big deal, you'll be in for a few days and then you'll be out. No one will even know," Pam told me.

Indeed, I had few options. They could commit me if they wished, but if I committed myself, I could leave when I wanted. I agreed to this, but not before we agreed on three conditions: no drugs, no shock treatment, and above all, the Holy Grail would remain in my possession for as long as I stayed there. They agreed.

I was now certain this was the best way to protect the Holy Grail. There were many advantages to this. In the institution, any behavior would be accepted, and hallucinations would be welcomed for as long as they were convinced I had a problem. In fact, what would not be expected would be for me to behave and talk in a "normal" manner. In the institution, I could continue to prepare the time capsule without being concerned about what people were thinking. I'd stay as long as it was to my advantage.

When Pam and I arrive at Our Lady of Mercy I saw that there were no bars on the windows, but when we got inside I discovered that they couldn't be opened. Their handles didn't even turn. I could also see the greenish color of the reinforced glass. There were no bars on the doors either, but just try to open them. They only opened from the outside, and the outside was always the side the patient wasn't on. When I passed through a door, I heard its lock click behind me. I was told that my room would be locked at night; in case of an emergency, they told me to press the red button on the wall next to the door.

The attendants watched everyone on monitors in the control room. There was a camera in every room, in the hallways, and in the common areas. The cameras dispatched them to where there was trouble.

In the dining and activity halls, two attendants were always posted in full view. Standing at the door in their white uniforms and with folded hands, they never moved their bodies, but their eyes were constantly moving, watching everything around them. In the common areas, the cameras constantly surveilled the room. Sometimes they stopped and zoomed in on a trouble maker or a subject who was under close observation—like I was.

Even the reception desk was monitored. There was a camera behind the receptionist, who was dressed in regular clothes rather than in a nurse's uniform. And she wouldn't let Pam come with me to help me settle in my room.

"Why don't you come next week during visit hours," she suggested.

"I'll come as soon as I can, darling. Let me know if you need anything," Pam told me before she left. I couldn't imagine what I could possibly need. I had the Holy Grail and the items for my time capsule packed away in my suitcase. This was all I needed.

If it wasn't for Dr. Green I could have enjoyed myself. There was an instant and mutual dislike between us. He was the psychiatrist I had to see every other day. He was also the one prescribing medication and administering shock therapies. The agreement I made before entering deprived him of using his two favorite tools. I could sense him thinking that he'd get me sooner or later. He'd try to trick me to break the rules, and then they could use that as an excuse to breach the agreement.

When I entered his office for our first session, Dr. Green managed to remain detached and aloof. He hardly spoke, and sometimes I wasn't sure if he was listening at all. He uttered sounds—hmmm. . . ya . . . go on—that must have been part of his professional training. His otherwise irritating silence intimidated me, making me feel like an insect under a magnifying glass. He was looking for double meanings or hidden motives behind everything. Every word had a hidden meaning that could reveal a subconscious secret. I felt I must always be on guard when I was around him.

"So," he said, "you have the Holy Grail?" A red light started flashing in my head. This couldn't be an innocent question.

"Yes," I answered, trying not to reveal my suspicions.

"Which one of the knights of the round table are you?" That was a trick question. I never thought I was one of the medieval knights, but I decided to answer and try to trip him up.

"Sir Galahad," I answered. That was the only possible answer. Sir Galahad was the only one who deserved to touch the Holy Grail. He was the most innocent of them all.

"Hmm . . . hmm," he said and made notes. "What do you intend to do with it?"

"To bring it to King Arthur of course." How cunning he was. I bet he expected me to say that I intended to drink from it so I would gain eternal life.

"Hmm . . . hmm . . ." He quickly made more notes.

For a long time he said nothing, trying to intimidate me with his silent treatment. I didn't say anything either.

I looked around. Finally, I asked if I could leave.

"The session isn't over yet," he told me. Then, after a few

minutes, he finally said, "Well?"

"Well what?"

"Have you anything else to say?"

"No."

"You can go now. I'll see you in two days."

"I heard you didn't cooperate with Dr. Green," Nancy told me later that day.

"Why? I participated. He gave me the silent treatment, and I didn't interrupt him."

Nancy smiled. She thinks I suffer from psychosis resulting from separation trauma. The loss of a mother at an early age surfaces from time to time in the form of hallucinations that replace true reality and compensate for the separations I have suffered. I keep trying to tell her that I don't imagine these things. They really happened. The world really changed, and I was there. But she has already made up her mind.

"Maybe I can see the Holy Grail?" Dr. Green asked in our next meeting.

"No."

"Why not?

"You're not a knight of pure heart."

"And you?"

"I am. I have the Holy Grail, don't I?"

"May I see another psychiatrist?" I asked Nancy later that day.

"No, he is the best, with a national reputation. Besides, he is also the medical director and the one who makes the case assignments."

So he was. Damn his reputation.

I restricted my interactions with the two of them to an absolute minimum; enough to enable me to stay there as long as I thought it would serve my purposes but not enough to be diagnosed as a more serious case. I cooperated with everyone, even Dr. Green. I didn't exhibit fits of temper or too deviant behavior; I also didn't mention my radiation sensitivity. Extreme behavior might result in more severe modes of treatment, like confinement, or even drug treatment and shock therapy. I knew those treatments could reduce a person to a benign, docile existence, like they most likely did to Terry.

It was Ginger, my nurse, who told me his name. In nice weather I'd see him pacing back and forth in a small fenced area outside; his hands were always folded behind his back, his shoulders slumped, and an expression of rage all over his face. His appearance and actions reminded me of an animal trapped in a cage. He was trying to get out, turning abruptly whenever he was stopped by the fence. It was there at every turn he made, but he never gave up his attempts. He tries again and again; only the observer could see how futile his efforts were. Terry reminded me of my recurring dream of walking along an endless plain. There was no fence in my dream, only the distant horizons that never got any closer, no matter how far I walked, and yet I continued to walk.

When I entered the activity hall for the first time, none of the forty or so other patients raised even an eyebrow in curiosity. Who cared? No one, not even the attendants at the door. The corner with the television was always occupied by the same four patients. Ginger told me they were the four J's, Joe, Jim, John, and Jack, but she didn't tell me what was wrong with them, only that they were war veterans. She couldn't remember which war though. The four J's didn't speak to each other. They sat silently in the corner watching television. Every morning they went directly to their corner, sat, and watched television until it was time to leave.

I preferred to sit alone and read when I was in the activity hall. Pam brought me fresh clothes and new magazines and books every week; however, I soon gave up reading because more significant events took place—events beyond the reach of all the Dr. Greens of the world, not even the monitors could detect what was happening.

I was watching television one night when suddenly the Holy Grail, resting in its usual place on top of it, began glowing with radiation. The radiation entered the set, and the screen began to grow larger. It continued growing, coming toward me, and I fled to a corner of the room. I was trapped. It grew until it was almost the size of the entire room. My heart was racing, and I was afraid that in a moment I would be crushed against the wall. I had no escape.

I extended my hands to try to push the television away from me, but they went right through it to the other side of the screen. I couldn't see them on the other side, but when I pulled them back, there they were. I put them through the screen again. I could still feel and move them, but I couldn't see them—at least I wouldn't be crushed by the television.

I was more curious than afraid now and wanted to see what was on the other side. I put my head in. What would happen if my entire body entered the other side of the screen? Before I could think up reasons for not doing it, I climbed through.

I found myself standing in front of a fast-food restaurant. It was a cloudy evening with light snow falling, and the golden glow from the restaurant's sign spread an enchanting yellow light on everything around it. My body and appearance had changed. I was twelve years old. This was my first date with Peggy! I had been quite nervous about the occasion. The electric charges I felt crawling along my back didn't come from the high voltage inside the television but from my nerves.

However, things were not completely as I remembered them. There were four sports cars in the parking lot. I saw the men who must be their owners inside the restaurant drinking coffee, and because it was cold, I decided to wait for Peggy inside.

As soon as I entered, the four men jumped up, knocking down everything in their way and spilling their coffee as they ran toward me.

"How do you like your hamburger?" they shouted, almost in unison. I was dumbfounded and couldn't speak for a moment. They kept repeating the question.

"Any way they come, I guess?" I finally managed to say.

"He's not the clown," said one of them.

Disappointed, they went up to the counter to get fresh cups of coffee. They looked familiar, but I couldn't place them anywhere. The man behind the counter also seemed familiar. His name tag said "Terry, Manager."

"What's the clown business all about?" I asked him. He was the manager so he must know what was going on.

"That's the reason they keep coming. There's a national contest. A clown is supposed to come to one of the restaurants, and the first person to ask the clown 'How do you like your hamburger?' will win the grand prize. They've come every single day since the contest began."

"Is the clown coming here?"

"Who knows. They definitely think so. Some kind of insider information. Are you going to order something?" I told him I was waiting for someone and would order later. "That's what they always say on cold days," he said and then resumed cleaning the spotless counter.

The four men were now watching a cartoon on a large television screen that was anchored close to the ceiling. I watched it with them while waiting for Peggy. The cartoon featured a male dancer with four arms that moved about as if they were made of rubber. He was juggling objects in the air. Occasionally his arms would wrap themselves around the objects, like the coils of a python, crushing them to dust. Then, he would pick other objects to dance with and then crush—this continued as if in a loop. In the background was an orchestra of cockroaches dressed in black forked coats.

The men sensed Peggy's approach and jumped up just before she entered the restaurant, just as they had done with me.

Like me, Peggy was surprised by the reception and unable to speak, but I came to her rescue.

"Leave her alone, she's not the clown," I shouted loudly.

Disappointed once again, they returned to their seats, but not before helping themselves to fresh cups of coffee.

"Are you all right?" I asked Peggy.

"I guess so . . . Yes, I'm okay. What's this all about?"

I told her everything that had happened since I arrived.

"Let's sit closer to the door," she suggested, "and we can beat them to the question when the clown arrives." I thought it was a great idea but wanted to order our food first.

"How do you like your hamburger?" I asked her.

"Without onions," she said.

"Impossible," said Terry, "our hamburgers always come with three rings of onion."

"What about making this one special, just for her?" Terry looked confused, unable to make a decision. He consulted his operating manual. "Can't," he said, finally coming to a decision, "but there's nothing in the manual saying you can't take the onion out yourself."

We ordered two hamburgers and fries. Peggy took out the onions, and then we started eating our hamburgers and dipping the fries into small puddles of ketchup. We didn't talk much.

"Come and join us," invited one of the four men. It was an unexpected gesture, which could only be due to our ability to beat them to the clown.

"Thank you, we're okay here."

"Come and join us here," he continued to insist until we

obliged.

"We are the four riders of the apocalypse," one of them said. This must have been an inside joke because they started to laugh. Peggy and I didn't find it funny but smiled politely anyway. Then, he stuck his hand into his jacket and stretched his neck, trying to look taller than he really was.

"I'm Joe the Conqueror, and this is Jim is the War Rider." Jim got up and bowed like an actor on stage, all while holding an invisible weapon of some kind.

"John here is the Greed Rider." John bowed, touching his forehead and chest with his hands while leaning forward. Then, he rubbed his fingers, like he was feeling money.

"Jack is the Death Rider." Jack growled at us and didn't get up.

"Peggy Taylor and Noah Miller," I stated matter-of-factly.

"Boyfriend and girlfriend," said John.

"Sweethearts," said Jim.

"Lovers," said Joe.

"Just friends," I said. Jack began laughing again, and the others joined him.

"I think we should leave," Peggy said, her face turning red.

"Don't get upset," Joe said, still struggling to control his laughter. "What kind of name is Noah anyway?" Obviously trying to change the subject. "Biblical? The guy who survived the flood?"

"Yes, with the ark and all the animals."

"And do you know who this is?" He said while pointing at Terry.

"He is Terry, the manager," I said.

"That's what he wants you to think, but really he is Hades, the gatekeeper."

"What gate? You mean the door of the restaurant?" I asked. It was an automatic door and opened whenever someone approached. They began to laugh again.

"No, not that. The gate to Hell."

"Oh." I didn't know how to respond.

"He follows us everywhere we go."

"Look here fellows, we don't really care who or what you are. We must be on our way now." I was ready to leave—the sooner the better.

"Don't you want to know?" Joe said as he leaned toward me.

"Know what?"

"We aren't really riders. We are four good drivers," he said. "We are four blessings bestowed on humanity. We stop the good from turning into evil. Indeed, the Bible describes the four horsemen of the apocalypse, four curses on the world, and we are the four virtues that go along with them."

"You drive to raise money for some cause?" I suggested, unsure what to make of this conversation.

They thought this was hilarious.

"We don't drive for a cause. We are the cause," Joe said when they stopped laughing.

"You play allegorical characters," said Peggy, "you aren't real people."

"They are the four blessings that humanity was cursed with," said Terry as he came out from behind the counter to join us.

"Like good turned evil?" Peggy ask.

"No. Good is evil by nature. It is absolute and uncompromising, thus it is worse than evil," Terry explained. "You see, God never cursed humanity, on the contrary, when Adam and Eve ate the fruit of knowledge, they became like him, knowing good and bad and able to tell them apart. He wanted to punish them but knew they were as knowledgeable as he was. So, God gave them four absolute, pure blessings, four destructive virtues—four imperatives. In this way, God outsmarted them, because such blessings are worse than curses. When their destructive nature isn't recognized, they are mistaken for true virtues."

"Like the Biblical Balaam who came to curse the children of Israel and ended up blessing them, but the blessing itself turned out to be a curse," Peggy replied. "She must be going to Sunday school,"

I thought to myself.

"Of course, we will never know what God's intentions were, to truly bless them or to curse them with such a blessing knowing their nature. He blessed them with the Ego, the human capacity for self-recognition, and the ability to distinguish between I and You." Joe explained and then inserted his fingers under his armpits and glared at us.

"That doesn't make any . . ." I start to say, but Joe interrupted me.

"You think that if you don't think you don't exist, which is why you are thinking all the time. But if you do or don't, it doesn't really matter. No one gives a damn. This is human ego, to think that the world was created for them . . ." he was interrupted by his pager. "My calling," he said and left.

"There goes the biggest ego of them all," Terry said.

On the television screen, there was now a program involving a large group of insects. Outside, I heard a car start and then the squeal of its tires as it sped away.

There was a brief silence after that, then Jim started to talk. He climbed up on the table next to us, bowed, and in a dramatic voice, as if in front of a large audience, recited a poem:

"The spider webs his net.

Man learns webbing but cannot web,

Without learning the spider webs.

How perfect is the spider's net?"

The other two applauded.

"Let's go. I'm sure the clown isn't coming," Peggy whispered into my ear.

"Not coming!? Speak up girl, how do you know? We must know how you came to such a conclusion."

"It's my intuition."

"Intuition doesn't count. It's not knowledge. It comes from the right half of the brain."

At this point, Jim's pager beeped.

"My calling," he said and left.

I heard another car start outside and then the squeal of tires.

Jack was the "compassion" driver, but Peggy kept interfering with his presentation, which was making him angry.

"Help the poor," he said.

"Maintain poverty to have poor people," Peggy said.

"Nurse the sick and help the wounded, help the hungry, shelter the homeless . . ."

"Wage wars to have wounded people in need, maintain food shortages to have the hungry, spend your resources on war implements," Peggy chimed in.

"Look here girl, if you keep interrupting . . ." But before he could say what would happen, his pager went off.

"My calling," he said and left.

Only John was left.

"I'm a humble handyman," said John, "I make things with my hands. I make factories . . ."

"And destroy the environment, assemble bombs, build nuclear weapons and gas chambers, build missiles . . ." Peggy interrupted.

"I also make other things. I make airplanes."

"And explosives to bring them down."

"And ships."

"And torpedoes to sink them."

Before this could go on for too long, his pager went off.

"My calling," he said and left.

We were sitting next to the entrance trying to regain our composure when two clowns entered. Their name tags said Don and Donna.

"How do you like your hamburger?" Peggy asked them.

"Any way they come," they answered.

"Do we have winners here tonight?" asked Don.

"We certainly do," Donna replied.

"Thank God it is over," Terry said.

CHAPTER 6

I had to go.

"Why don't you stay until we get our prize?" Peggy asked.

As much as I wanted to stay, I couldn't. I needed to get back to the other side of the screen. There might be a time difference between the two sides. I had already been inside the screen for two hours by my estimation, and I needed to be cautious. Any moment now Ginger might be coming to wake me up to start the daily routines. If she doesn't find me, it will be impossible for me to explain where I was, or even worse, I could emerge from the screen while she is in my room.

"I must go, but I'll be back as soon as I can."

We didn't kiss goodbye. I shook her hand and left.

I wasn't sure about finding my way back. That, however, turned out to be easier than I expected. I followed my footprints, which were still visible in the snow, until I found a black rectangle the size of a large television screen. This was the threshold separating the two sides. I put my hand through, and, just like before, it disappeared into the other side. I stuck my head in to see where this threshold would take me, and I saw my room. I climbed back over. The Holy Grail was on the television where I had left it, and it wasn't emitting radiation anymore. I soon discovered that hardly any time had passed. What seemed to me like a couple of hours inside the television was only a couple of minutes on this side, less time than it took for one commercial.

"You must have fallen asleep with the television on," said Ginger, turning it off when she came in the morning.

It was going to be one of those long tedious days, and Ginger suggested I go to the activity hall. I arrived there to find the four J's in their corner, as usual, sitting in front of the television watching cartoons. Now I recognized them, they were the four drivers from the restaurant!

I tried to catch their eyes and see if they recognized me. They continued to gaze at the screen. Perhaps they would have reacted if they knew I beat them to the prize, but they couldn't know that yet.

The nurses were encouraged to eat with the patients. It gave an illusion of a large happy family eating together. Ginger often sat with me, and I didn't mind. I liked her.

"How do you like your hamburger?" Ginger asked me. My heart skipped a beat and then began racing like crazy. This was the clowns' question! Inside the television, this was the question that could win you the grand prize. Was Ginger also in on this, or was it just an innocent question?

"Any way they come," I replied, giving the clowns' answer. If she was in on it, she would recognize this response. Ginger's face didn't show any indication that she recognized my response. I began laughing hysterically to relieve my tension.

"What's so funny?"

"Nothing. I'm sorry, but I can't stand the pretense of having a choice when in fact there is none. Hamburgers here come only one way. It is part of a game, asking you what you want, and you end up getting the same no matter what."

"I like mine with everything on it and lots of ketchup," she said. Now we both laughed, and in spite of my poor appetite, I ate my hamburger with lots of ketchup.

There was nothing about our interactions that would suggest to an outsider that most of the people here suffered from some sort of mental affliction, or any other affliction for that matter. Everyone can be judged as crazy under certain circumstances—provided there is the right diagnosis. In my case, they used a specific book to diagnose me as suffering from obsession with an object, the Holy

Grail, a fetish as they call it, to which I attached supernatural powers.

"The subject claims to be able to see radiation. The subject is colorblind." Fortunately, they think separating the subject—me—from the object of his obsession—the Holy Grail—may result in severe trauma. How is that for a security blanket? "Like the loss of the subject's mother when he was an infant." How ingenious. "Onset: loss of mother. Prognosis: moderate to good."

How do I know all this? Simple, I read a few psychology books before coming here. How else could I present the right symptoms? I also know that at some point in my "recovery" they'll decide I no longer need my security blanket and can do without it. My lack of suffering from another separation trauma will be an indication of my recovery. Fortunately, such separation at present would be traumatic.

Judging someone to be delusional is also a matter of degrees. If I am the only person who can see radiation colors, it's madness, but if multiple pilgrims see a wooden idol shed tears of blood, it's a religious experience. When I see the Holy Grail radiate and transform the world, it's a hallucination, but when prophets swear to have seen God riding in a chariot of fire, it's mythology.

"Has the Holy Grail been active?" asked Dr. Green, not even saying hello, how do you do, or sit down. I sat anyway. Today the question felt threatening, and I was afraid he would find out that there was something on my mind—which was to get the hell out of here as soon as possible and go back to the restaurant where the prize was about to be awarded.

"Some," I said. Nancy had asked me the same question earlier today, and I told her the Holy Grail was not active. There was no better strategy for me than to keep them confused at all times. Their books don't deal with inconsistent information. As usual, Dr. Green was taking notes and didn't respond.

"But it will be active tonight." I continued.

"How do you know?"

"Last night I met the four riders of the apocalypse, and they told me so."

"May I come and watch?" he asked as his pen raced across his notepad.

"Not unless you are one of the knights of the roundtable."

After this response, Dr. Green changed the subject. "It's stolen property, you know. It belongs to the Met." This truly enraged me, and it was good for giving the right impression. It was still too early to separate me from the Holy Grail.

"It's a holy object, and as such, it's not anyone's property." His pen was racing like crazy after I stated this, maybe prescribing me some medication in spite of the agreement I made with them. I couldn't trust him.

"That will be all for today," he said suddenly. This was my shortest session with him—maybe another of the Holy Grail's miracles.

As the day dragged toward evening, I waited impatiently to hear Ginger lock my door for the night. After this I would be free to go back and look for the restaurant where the clowns were, claim my prize, and continue my date with Peggy.

However, I did have doubts that I could return. After I finally heard Ginger lock the door, I placed the Holy Grail on top of the television and turned it on, not sure what to expect; the radiation resumed, going into the set just like the previous night. When I turned the set off the radiation ceased; on again, and the radiation resumed. Hallelujah, now I could activate the Holy Grail at will; the two appeared to be linked.

I discovered I could pick a channel, place the Holy Grail on the television, and then enter that program. What an experience. All I had to do to join the action was to step across the screen, the threshold to the other side. But I was searching for a particular place and time: I was searching for last night at the restaurant, where the clowns were about to reward me and Peggy the grand prize for the national hamburger contest.

Many of the channels tempted me to step into them—the

four musketeers defending their queen and mastering the art of dueling, Billy the Kid's gang of four robbing banks, Roman legions defeating armies of slaves, knights of the roundtable besieging a castle, pirates ransacking a Spanish galleon, an army of robots blasting other humanoids with conventional weapons—but I finally came upon one channel that looked like it might be the one from last night. I couldn't tell whether it was the same or not, but I took a chance and stepped across the screen.

Everything was the same as when I left. I had been away for a whole day, but it had only been a blink of the eye here. No one even noticed I had gone away.

"I thought you had to leave," Peggy said.

"I changed my mind," I replied. I didn't mention how I'd already gone and returned.

The clowns were both wearing oversized floppy shoes. Their faces were painted white; Don had a large laughing mouth, while Donna's was a bleak, sad one. Large, shiny red noses dominated their faces, and around their necks they had large bowties with blinking lights. Donna wore a tall orange conical hat with a bell at its tip, and she had on a blue minidress and green tights with yellow polka dots. Don was wearing a shaggy red wig and red t-shirt, and his oversized purple pantaloons were held in place by pink suspenders. I wouldn't vouch to guess what those colors would look like to someone else.

Those were the colors I saw with my radiation-sensitive vision.

Before the award ceremony could start, they had to decorate the restaurant—hanging balloons, paper chains, posters with their pictures on them, and many ribbons—and soon the place looked like it was ready for a child's party. In spite of the festivity around him, Terry seemed to be in a bad mood.

"Aren't you glad this is all over with?" I asked him, thinking he would be glad to have the contest behind him.

"It's unfair," he said. "The four drivers came here every day, waiting for the clowns to come, and then you and that girl walk in for the first time and win."

"If we don't get the prize that would be unfair," said Peggy.

We sat at the table, waiting. Not knowing what the prize was added excitement to the whole affair.

Finally, Don opened the bag he had been carrying with him, and took some green plastic insects out of it.

"Super insects," he said. I saw nothing special about them, super or not.

"One doesn't need to have super vision to see these are not ordinary insects," Donna said. I was surprised to hear her alluding to my radiation vision; she couldn't possibly know about it.

"Clowns know all," she said, reading my mind. "The super insects are made of plastic, which is solidified chunks of petrol."

"So?"

"Chunks of energy."

On the television there was now an educational program about super insects.

"What is this all about?" Peggy asked.

"These are the winner's prizes. You can each pick one insect."

"This is the grand prize?" I was deeply disappointed. "I don't want a bug."

"Neither do I," Peggy said.

"Like it or not, you must take one. These are the prizes."

"You can keep your lousy bugs; we don't want any of them." I pictured those four guys coming back to find out they were coming here every day to win a lousy plastic insect. Quite a disappointment.

"They're super insects, not bugs. Those who know about them would appreciate the value of this prize," said Donna. "They're made of plastic, you know."

"Solidified petrol is solidified chunks of energy," said Don, perhaps thinking that repeated a second time, the information would impress us.

On the screen there was a parade of insects, thousands of different kinds marching in an endless line. "Like all other organic matter, super insects are chunks of solidified sun energy," the narrator explained.

"These are models of those super insects," Donna informed us. Now that we were better informed, maybe we'd accept the prizes.

"We still don't want them."

The screen now featured a colony of super ants.

"Ants are all identical, none of them possess anything the others don't. They share all their knowledge equally, and when one of them dies, nothing is lost. Each one has complete and total knowledge. When an individual human dies, this knowledge is lost, because every human has unique knowledge and private experiences. This is why human knowledge is never complete," the narrator on the screen continued.

"That makes no sense," I said.

"Here, you may like this instead." Don offered me a pair of diddle bobbers, a headband with two antennas attached, which bobbed up and down when placed on your head, and he handed Peggy a bottle of Bubble Bee Soap Bubbles Solution, which she gave to me to hold onto.

I decided I would add the diddle bobbers and the bottle of Bubble Bee Soap Bubbles Solution to my time capsule.

CHAPTER 7

After I returned to my room, I lay in bed thinking. There must be some significance to the prizes. The diddle bobbers must be more than what they appear. When I thought I had finally figured out the answer to this riddle, I fell asleep.

In the morning I decided to pretend to be an ant and wore the diddle bobbers on my head. No one questioned how I got them, all they worried about was the setback in my condition. Maybe they assumed I had brought the diddle bobbers with me in my suitcase.

They considered it a major setback, but I didn't care. I was determined to find out if the diddle bobbers could serve as antennas. Could they receive messages like insects' antennas did? Moments before I drifted off to sleep last night I had come to the realization that they must have such capabilities, and I was determined to listen and discover their secret. If it was a useless toy, why would the clowns have given it to me? I was determined to find out what purpose the diddle bobbers served and what messages they would receive.

"But why an ant?" Pam asked when she came to visit that afternoon. I wished she hadn't come. She had been crying, and her eyes were still red. I don't know what they told her. The damage had been done, and I was committed to this charade, no matter how much it hurt her. I was determined to unravel the riddle of the diddle bobbers. I was certain there was a great secret in them.

"Because they are the most perfect creatures," I told her. I didn't want to upset her even more by telling her about the adventures in the television.

"But why? What does this have to do with you? With us?"

"Their antennas are tuned to receive the universal message."

"What is that message?"

"Only the insects know and understand it."

"And you want to hear it?"

"If I'm deserving."

"Are you?"

"I'll be ready when it comes," I said with conviction. But her question did raise some doubts in my mind. I didn't know when and how often such messages might come. Did they come all the time or only occasionally? Above all, maybe the diddle bobbers were fake, incapable of receiving the universal message.

"Why do you care about ants so much now?" Pam was visibly getting more upset.

"Maybe it's time we should all care about them. Maybe the world would be a better place if we did." Pam was unable to contain her tears, and I was truly sorry for the pain I caused her—sorry for both of us. But this was only a temporary situation, and I was sure that when I told her the full story she'd understand.

Pam left without saying another word. She didn't even kiss me goodbye.

"Why an ant and not a bee, for example?" Nancy asked later, during our daily session.

"I am protesting the dismal and abusive treatment ants have received."

Nancy wanted to know more about this, and I was more than eager to share with her what I had learned from the clowns, even though I doubted she had any genuine interest. Maybe it was the diddle bobbers that gave me the inspiration; maybe this was part of the universal message.

"We commemorate much lesser causes, why not ants? We commemorate paper documents, pieces of cloth we call flags, statues or other idols, and all kinds of past events, while we mistreat ants. Just think about the pesticides we use to exterminate them. And do you hear them protest? Do you know why not? Because they improved and became super ants." I was wasting my time explaining this to her.

"It is ridiculous for an adult to wear such a childish contraption," she said.

"Elsewhere, perhaps, but not here."

She gave me a look, as if she could see through my charade. "In what way are ants superior?" she asked.

"Have you ever seen one ant kill another one just for pleasure, or steal, or commit any other senseless crime? They never covet power or any material possessions. They never steal or kill because none of them lack what the others have. All they have, they have equally, or none of them have it. They live in a utopic society, surpassing any envisioned by humans. It is just natural to them. They don't have laws or commandments because they don't need them. The ants quietly achieved what is coveted by all other species. They live in complete harmony with the world and move in step with it. In each one of them is the entire mystery of the world. They have permanent pleasure, fulfillment, and contentment." I was getting carried away and proceeded to tell her everything I had learned from the clowns and the educational television show playing on the screen in the restaurant, but I never mentioned the clowns.

"This sounds like a dull existence."

"By human standards, perhaps. Ant life is the pure joy of living. They live like they're in a state of permanent orgasm, which requires no effort, no self, and no partners."

"And by wearing those antennas you will achieve all this?"

"Maybe yes, maybe no, and maybe in my next life I will be privileged enough to be a real ant."

"Reincarnated as an ant?"

"Who knows? There's no way of telling."

Later, I saw Dr. Green. In spite of my agreement, he prescribed me medication. He also wanted to hear about the ants.

"Their divine mother is the source of their life. She is the key to their superiority," I said, and I also told him everything I told Nancy. Dr. Green raised his right eyebrow.

"Well," he said after some time.

"Well . . ." I said, and continued, "They don't have the pleasure of sex." Sex was something psychiatrists used to try to explain away many human problems. I was so eager to talk about the ants and develop my theory that I didn't care I was talking to Dr. Green. "They don't need such pleasure because they live in a constant state of ecstasy, which cannot be surpassed by any temporal pleasures. They delegated the procreation functions to their divine mother and with it the gratification of temporal sexual pleasures. Through that brief encounter, their parents combined and gave them life. The divine mother was impregnated with the life of their divine father, who perished and gave his life power to them so they could come into being. By doing so, he gives them eternal life."

"Ants die, you know."

"Individually, yes, but each of them being identical to the others, nothing is lost. None of them possess or know anything the others don't, and their individual death has no consequences for their continued existence as a species. The temporal is the source of the eternal. And the eternal begets the temporal."

Dr. Green abruptly ended our session.

The other residents showed no interest in the diddle bobbers. The four J's were in their corner, and each of them was holding a piece of string with a green plastic insect tied at the end. This couldn't be a coincidence, the television world must have powers on both sides of the screen. I asked Ginger about these insects.

"A new therapeutic approach; caring for a pet can bring them out of their shells."

"It makes more sense than having a pet rock, but still, the insects aren't alive."

"It makes no difference, this is an experimental approach."

The four J's got their prizes after all. Maybe that was the reason they weren't mad at me.

"I can get you one."

"No, thanks. What kind of insects are they?"

"I don't know, a superb kind no doubt, they eat nothing and are made of plastic." She meant it as a joke but didn't know how close to the truth she was.

As evening approached, my frustration and disillusion grew. I hadn't heard the universal message; I hadn't heard any transmissions for that matter. The diddle bobbers might be nothing more than an inferior imitation of insects' antennas after all. I had no inclination to keep talking about ants or any other insect. Insects don't speak, do they? As an ant, it was easy for me to maintain my silence for the rest of the day.

I was in bed and ready to take the diddle bobbers off when the Holy Grail started to radiate. The room was filled with glowing light. The television was off, and the radiation spread around. I was engulfed in light. Suddenly, everything turned dark, and all the radiation condensed into a narrow stream of energy that entered my antennas and activated them.

The walls melted away in the darkness, and the room expanded. Black spots appeared, like an army of ants marching in every direction and crawling into me. In the darkness there was a deep silence; this was the sound of the world.

I was breathing a different type of air in the darkness, and it was crisp and pure, like an ocean breeze, intoxicating me. My chest was moving up and down with the flow of the air. It came into me, filling me. At first, I observed the flow of the air and was aware of my breathing. Gradually, its pureness overwhelmed me, and the air was breathing for me, coming inside and out of me by itself. Each breath of air was identical to the previous one and yet different, like a stream of black ants, each identical to the others and different from them. There was now only pure breathing and nothing else.

I experienced eternity. All worldly time converged into this single cosmic moment in which all pasts and futures combined. Everything that had ever existed returned to its source: the primordial black hole.

As I sunk deeper toward its center, I became aware of myself. For an instant, I was afraid I wouldn't be able to separate from it. This is the awareness that distinguishes humans from insects, who are aware of nothing. I reached toward the diddle bobbers, trying to remove them, but my hand was jolted by an electrical charge. I dissolved into the darkness.

When I regained consciousness I was at the foot of a tall hill that had a winding trail leading up to the top. I didn't know where the hill was or why I was here. Next to me there was an old rusty sign swaying in the breeze. It had "Hill 537" written on it and an arrow that pointed in different directions with every gust of wind. Occasionally it pointed toward the trail.

In front of me there were two large rocks that looked like the pillars to a gate entrance or doorway, but there was no fence or wall. I walked through them and suddenly saw a large tree at the top of the hill. It wasn't a special tree. It reminded me of the tree in my backyard where my dad built me a treehouse; I played many childhood games there. This tree could have been a maple, oak, tulip, or apple tree. It was all of them—it was a universal tree.

It was used to build our dining table. It burned to ashes in our fireplace. It was the tree of life. It was the tree of knowledge and the tree of good and evil. It was the firewood on Isaac's altar. It was a tree whose name I didn't know.

I looked around. The entire hill was full of energy waves moving in every direction. Everything was distorted, vibrating, and twisting; the entire space was swollen with energy and ready to explode. The spears of grass moved in waves, like the snakes on Medusa's head. Warm air simmered up, swollen with energy, and cool air filtered down to be recharged.

The tree was moving, and suddenly it changed shape. It turned into the figure of a man with four arms, a dancer. It was constantly transforming, becoming a human figure and then changing back into a tree; a cosmic loop. Once, the dancer danced around the hill before changing back into a tree.

The other objects on the hill were also shifting their shapes.

The blades of grass, flowers, and insects merged with the dancer, then separated from him. They joined with him, then they moved by themselves in their original forms, and the dancer danced among the objects, oblivious to them. His dance had no form, and he followed no rules.

Sometimes he moved slowly and gracefully, and the objects around him slowed down with him. His four arms moved as if he was made from rubber, making waves flow down the length of each of them. Other times, he danced in leaps and strides, jumping without any gravity to hold him down, and the dance changed into the ecstasy of a storm, with his hands quivering like grass in a strong wind. Soon, the dance was so fast he appeared frozen in place.

He was Shiva, the prince of dancers, and the dance was the source of the energy that set the world in motion. The energy surged and spread around him, like ripples on a pond, and all matter danced with him—tiny specks of dust and galaxies all danced in unison with him, distant pulsars vibrated to his rhythm.

Then, I saw his energy penetrate atoms, reaching to their center. Protons, neutrons, and electrons all joined the glorious dance and started to move; in straight lines and in curves, as fast as light travels, vibrating like waves and bouncing like balls, dancing and colliding, changing and transforming into the more elementary particles from which they were composed. The more elementary they became, the more complex they were, and their ends were their beginnings.

The energy now radiated at every length and frequency of the electromagnetic spectrum. I saw all the waves and frequencies combine: wave crests combined with their troughs, canceling each other out, peaks combined with bottoms, creating one mighty universal energy field, high frequencies combined with low, short with long, until they all became one flat wave of enormous energy. Shiva's stormy, glorious dance had subsided, and now it was tranquil and quiet.

Was this the power of the diddle bobbers? Or was this the Holy Grail?

I woke up in the morning dreading my session with Nancy that afternoon. I was still overwhelmed by my experience and didn't feel like talking to anyone. When I went to Nancy's office, the secretary wasn't outside at the desk. The door to her office was ajar, and I heard Nancy talking with Dr. Green about me.

". . . the medication I gave him needs more time to take effect, although there is already some improvement." My little triumph. I had tricked the conniving doctor. I only pretended to take the medication, holding it under my tongue and then spitting it out later when no one was watching.

"I don't think he needs any medication."

"He isn't an ant today, is he? To what else would you ascribe this change? To a miraculous recovery?"

"You know medication doesn't work after just one day. In fact," said Nancy, "I don't think he needs it at all. I wouldn't be surprised if he is putting us all on. There is too much method to his madness. Fetish, yes. But the rest of it is a pretense."

"Being an ant was a masquerade?"

"Yes," she insisted, her voice carrying conviction, "It is all too well structured and thought out. It makes too much sense. It isn't spontaneous. Even if he tries to make us believe his experiences are real, he knows very well that the visions are not, perhaps they are nothing more than a dream. I would wager he knows the boundaries between reality and his so-called visions quite well. Vivid imagination I would say, or some game he plays. Sometimes, I am ready to swear there is nothing wrong with him in the clinical sense."

I began to worry.

"I think," she continued, "his childhood accident create some type of neurological change in his brain, like short-circuiting the connections. The result is that he sees two parallel realities that don't interfere with each other. One is real and the other is the same reality seen through memories, ideas, and fears. One is the right half of the brain and the other is the left. When push comes to shove, he can distinguish between them. He functions well in family life and at work."

"And the Holy Grail, as he calls that ridiculous cup, how do you account for that?"

"I can't. This is one thing I still can't fit into my theory. Not all the details fit yet. But sometimes I feel he does it all on purpose, to confuse us. He seems to move without difficulty from one reality to another. Sometimes he gives the impression that he has no control over it, attributing it to that cup, but other times, I get the impression that he does control it. Both realities are populated with the same people . . . people from his past, like Peggy, for example."

Those were all interesting theories, but I didn't agree with them. My visions, as she calls them, are real, and they can't be explained away by some textbook theories. There were too many facts she didn't know about, like crossing into the television.

"Enough of this! He must continue with the medication, and tell Ginger to make sure he really takes it. If that doesn't work, we'll see about other means."

Dr. Green left the office in a hurry, not paying attention to me waiting there.

I was uncooperative during the session with Nancy, and, for the rest of the day, I felt that my carefully planned scheme was about to fall apart.

Later in my room, as I gazed absentmindedly at the television, I automatically put on the diddle bobbers.

CHAPTER 8

Hordes of children were on the march, passing over the land like human locusts, devastating the landscape. Nothing could stand in their way. They were dressed in rags, some waving assault rifles and others carrying rocket launchers. They left behind only flat, bare land, shearing it of anything that grew or was built on it. Whatever obstacle they encountered, they dismantled it and carried it away, piece by piece, like ants carrying grains of wheat. Maybe this was what created the plain in my dream.

I didn't change channels. During a break I saw a commercial for a Laser Beam Gun. It was the same model I had received for my twelfth birthday.

Dad told me that weapons—even toy ones—teach violence and disregard for human life, therefore I wasn't allowed to play with them. But I still begged for a Laser Beam Gun for my birthday. I was the only child on the block who didn't have one. I could play with them at friends' houses, but no one wanted to come to play with my toys, so I learned to use them in creative ways: a tractor, with some imagination, could function as a tank, and the peaceful town I built with my building blocks—with its churches, shops, and quiet streets—could be turned into a battlefield. Despite my creativity, I still dreamed of owning a Laser Beam Gun. It was Lou who finally persuaded Dad to buy it for me. It was wrapped in gift paper and placed among the other birthday gifts, but I recognized it even before I opened the package.

I extended my hand into the television to hold the Laser Beam Gun, but my hand closed on empty space. When I climbed into the screen I was in our old living room, and on the floor in front of me was my old Laser Beam Gun.

I left the house to meet my friends; we were all members of the Space Warriors. We had a secret base on the hill just past Lovers Lane. There was a treehouse there and other structures that we built from branches or pieces of lumber we had scavenged. Sometimes we would bring old blankets and make army-style tents.

We had sworn an oath to always be friends and loyal to each other, even if captured by the enemy and tortured. The ceremony had taken place in the treehouse, We placed our right hands on our

Laser Beam Guns and swore allegiance to the order of the Space Warriors.

Our enemies were the Galaxy Knights, the children from the neighboring subdivision. Until all this knight business got into their heads, they used to be a decent bunch of kids. I even had a few friends among them.

At the beginning of the conflict between us, we agreed on some ground rules. The "Articles of War," as we called them, spelled out things to do and not to do and outlined the rules for when a warrior was killed. What could be simpler? But when it came to it, they never admitted to being killed, denying the laser beam touched them, that it was only a flashlight, or other such outrageous lies. They forced us to lie like them. You can't fight an enemy who never dies. What I hated most about the so-called Galaxy Knights was that they forced others to lower themselves to their level.

Our commander was Dan, my best friend. He had a laser sword that not only shone green light but also emitted electric sparks and made electronic sounds on impact. His high-energy particle gun could shoot neutron darts.

We reached Base X but didn't expect the Galaxy Knights to attack that day. We assumed defense positions around the hill; today was a drill. We charged into the woods, shooting until only the trees and a few rocks remained. The enemy was defeated. We had won.

We were laughing and joking and were very happy with our victory, in a way that only children could be. I was running around in circles with my hands extended to the sides, like the wings of an airplane. Then, I was spinning around faster and faster until I got dizzy and was ejected out onto the other side of the television due to the speed of my spin.

A bee was ejected with me. How scared she must have been to suddenly find herself away from the hill, its flowers, and her fellow bees. She followed me all that day, and no wonder; in this strange place, I was her only connection to her home. She stayed near me to make sure she'd be able to return with me. Soon, however, the bee had fun. In the activity hall the residents started to shout and yell, agitated by the harmless little creature who wasn't even a killer bee. Two attendants chased her with folded magazines, but she eluded them. She hid, then came back as soon as everyone was certain she had escaped through the open window, and the fiasco of the chase repeated itself.

I thought the bee was an opportunity for me to tell Nancy about the other side of the television screen. In our next session I told her about my adventures on the other side of the television. Nancy responded with skepticism. I was disappointed. I had hoped she would be more open-minded and understand that the bee was proof that I was not imagining things.

"Is a white-clad Our Lady of Mercy attendant more real than Peggy and the clowns at the fast-food restaurant?" I asked.

Nancy was quiet for a while.

"Maybe you are right."

"And the bee, isn't she real?" I once more brought up what I thought to be my most decisive argument.

"The bee could have come from anywhere."

After I left Nancy's office I tried to communicate with the bee. I put on the diddle bobbers, but all the bee did was sit on one of the bobbers, stroking it with her antennas. Maybe she had nothing to say, or perhaps she was too scared to say anything in this strange environment.

When evening came, I searched among the channels to find my friends, but I couldn't find them. Finally, I gave up and stepped into a place that resembled my childhood Base X. There was a tall hill, soaring well above the other hills in the distance. There was also a thick forest around this hill, and a giant tree on top of it.

"Where have you been?" Dan asked as soon as I climbed through, landing between two large rocks near the giant tree on top of the hill. I hadn't expected to be back with my friends. "And what the hell is the matter with you?"

I was wearing jeans, a t-shirt, and sneakers. My friends were now in their early twenties and part of an army unit. They were wearing army fatigues and steel helmets and were carrying rifles, grenades, and other weapons.

Some of them were snickering, then there was an avalanche of laughter. I laughed with them, but I was quite nervous about all this and didn't know what I was laughing about.

"It's a clever stunt," said Dan. "Where did you get this ridiculous outfit anyway?"

They weren't aware of the other side of the screen any more than those on the outside were aware of this side. To them, this was the only world that existed, and like on the other side, they'd think I was off-center if I mentioned the existence of a different reality.

Someone gave me a rifle and army fatigues to wear, but the clothes were too big for me.

I wondered about the bee. I didn't see her come back with me but saw many bees flying around searching for flowers on this hill. Then I saw the harmony that existed on the hill. Everything was connected, only the soldiers didn't actually belong here. The hill existed despite them and ignored them as long as they didn't interfere with the life of the hill. The hill was at peace with itself and the universal energy field. The atmosphere gave off a serene, well-balanced energy. Here, in this delicate harmony, the smallest shift in energy could result in turmoil. The balance of the universal energy field could be shattered to pieces by anything disruptive, like a bullet.

I tried not to think about bullets, but then I heard one passing over our heads with a high pitch sound, like a giant killer bee. It sank into the trunk of the giant tree. This was followed by the sound of a shot from the direction of the forest. The actual sequence of events was in reverse: the shot should have been first, then the bullet passing over us and sinking into the tree. Everyone froze in place. This was completely unexpected. But I stayed calm. I knew why this happened; I was able to make the things I imagined appear in this world.

Panic ensued. Everyone started shouting and running in different directions. When the commotion subsided, everyone—except for me—was under cover and had assumed defensive positions. More shots came.

I lay behind a small rock next to Dan, who was scanning the woods with binoculars. Randy came running toward us, struggling to pull up his pants—the shooting had disturbed his call of nature on the far side of the hill.

"What's going on?" he asked.

"Get down!" Dan ordered.

"If I knew there was going to be a war, I wouldn't have come. I want to go home." Randy began to cry. He was scared, and I was embarrassed to see him like this.

"Let him go," I told Dan. He didn't respond. Randy kept crying.

On Dan's map, our location was labeled hill 537. Dan told me it is an important strategic location in the Matilda Mountains. Where are the Matilda Mountains? Who was the enemy?

Randy was still sobbing when we saw heavy smoke rising in the distance.

"There go our replacements and supplies."

We were surrounded. Randy couldn't go home now.

Mike was the first one killed. He got up, defying the bullets around us, waving his gun above his head, and daring the enemy.

"Get down, you idiot!" Dan yelled.

"Death to the Galaxy Knights!" Mike shouted at the enemy and then took two steps backward as if pushed by an invisible force, and dropped to the ground while clutching his chest. What a performance!

Some of the soldiers giggled, but I didn't. I knew what had really happened. Others clapped their hands; they were expecting Mike to get up and bow, like an actor receiving his reward. But when he didn't get up, the giggles turned into nervous laughter and then stopped.

The life of the hill continued undisturbed through all of this. The human battle intensified, but it didn't interrupt the life of the hill. The flowers and the green grass kept swaying softly in the light breeze. The air was full of many different kinds of insects, and others were crawling on the ground. Butterflies moved gracefully through the air, leaving no trace behind them. Bees were buzzing around looking for nectar, streams of black ants followed the trails leading to and from their underground homes, and grasshoppers hopped and jumped from one place to another, momentarily disturbing the grass where they landed. It was a world in harmony, oblivious to the raging battle.

The first bullet had struck the tree and sunk into its trunk. I saw where it had hit and thought that it would be a nice item to add to my time capsule, so I got up to dig the bullet out of the tree.

"Get down you idiot." Dan repeated, alarmed to see me walking among the flying bullets. I wasn't trying to be a hero, but this was my illusion, and I didn't think the bullets could kill me.

I soon discovered that I couldn't control events once they started. I could start them, but then they assumed their own course, like tuning into a show but having no control over it other than selecting the channel.

With my pocket knife I began digging the slug out. I cut around it, going deep into the trunk and causing more damage than the bullet. I finally uncovered it and continued to cut away at the trunk until it came loose and fell into my hand.

The battle was getting out of control, but I couldn't do anything to stop it, even though I tried to think about pleasanter things. Tom was killed next, then Alex. He was hit when he got up to look for a more comfortable spot to take cover.

Ants were now crawling on him, and he was lying on his back with his eyes wide open, like he was trying to see as much as he could during his last moments. Maybe he saw the flowers and insects. Maybe he saw the universal energy field and the hill's wonderful harmony. Or maybe his eyes were simply open in surprise.

I saw a bee land on a yellow flower and walk down one of the petals, following a vein that led her to the dark center where there was a patch of dark fuzz. The bee inserted her head into the flower's center. Her belly began moving up and down to the rhythm of the universal energy field. It was the rhythm of cosmic intercourse. The flower responded and began to move, slowly at first, then more vigorously until its stalk vibrated and shook with an ecstatic intensity as it reached its cosmic orgasm. The stalk shook the stem, and they spread golden pollen on the bee. Slowly, the ecstasy subsided, and the bee flew away, covered in golden dust and carrying the flower's nectar.

The pollen impregnated the flower. I saw its petals dry up, fall, and then new ones grow to cover the flower's naked center. The cells inside began to split and multiply until they grew into a piece of fruit that was full of seeds.

The fruit drew energy from the universal energy field, ripened, and then burst open to free the seeds. A light wind came and carried them away. I saw the seed falling on the hill, sprouting, and sending roots into the ground. Leaves came out, and new flowers bloomed, covering the hill in a rainbow of colors.

CHAPTER 9

The other side of the television screen had mesmerized me. I was lured into it every night now, unable to resist its powerful call. Things there were thrilling and unexpected. Events often took bizarre turns and were not bound by the rules of time and space. None of the fundamental rules of outside reality applied there. Reactions did not always follow actions, and effects could happen before their causes, consequences before their reasons, and later events before those that preceded them. Time could be sped up or slowed down, space could reach beyond its boundaries, and events separated by great expanses of time could happen side by side there. Even if it followed some rules, I didn't know what they were, and they could change from one show to another. I liked it this way—it kept the suspense and surprise alive.

The more I crossed the screen, the greater the hold it had over me, but I was still aware of where I truly belonged. I could leave at any time I wished. I had free will and could cross the threshold that separated the two worlds at will.

Lately, my stay on the outside was getting more annoying. Outside the screen, I had to obey their rules, play their games, and live according to their expectations in the *real* world.

***

The morning after I witnessed the life of the hill, I woke up in my room, curled up like a baby on the floor. Judging from my aching body, I must have been there for some time. Afraid Ginger would find me on the floor this way, I got up and climbed into bed.

That evening I returned to the hill. I arrived just as there was a lull in the battle. This silence was more frightening than the shooting. The enemy might be regrouping to assault us or retreating to attack us with some terrible weapons.

A new sound could be heard in the distance. It was the dull sound of approaching helicopters. Dan scanned the sky with his binoculars, and I saw a wide smile spread across his face. Two blue and white NTN World Tonight News helicopters were coming. I had just been thinking about video cameras and taping the hill and the battle so I would have irrefutable evidence to show Nancy and Dr. Green!

"We're going to be on NTN national television, our lucky stars," Dan said excitedly.

As the helicopters came closer, everyone stood up, cheering and waving their hands as the helicopters started to circle the hill to land. After they landed, raising clouds of dust, out came the news team, headed by the celebrity reporter Ned Carmichael. He could say things with such authority that everyone believed him, no matter what he said—it became authoritative truth and undisputed fact. We gathered around the helicopters, watching the crew unload their equipment. There was no danger now, and we could walk around freely.

"Testing, 1, 2, 3 . . . testing . . ." said someone on the camera crew. The news crew had just finished setting up their equipment, but Carmichael was upset.

"Now that you're finally finished, we can start and get away from this dump," he said to them.

"You're on air," said a cameraman, pointing his finger at the news anchor. Carmichael's expression instantly changed. On camera he was different, a pleasant man.

"This is Ned Carmichael. I am speaking to you live from hill 537, a place most of you haven't heard of and will not be able to locate on a map."

Dan fired a green flare, signaling the battle to resume. The soldiers hurried back to their places, and soon, the air was once more filled with flying bullets and gunfire. A real battle was taking place.

Carmichael continued his report, and what he reported became the truth, regardless of the facts. "Nothing really takes place unless it is reported, and it is I who reports it" was his favorite statement. The skirmish on the hill couldn't have come at a better time.

I wondered how Carmichael could deliver the broadcast in such a casual yet authoritative manner, without any slips of the tongue or hesitations. And then, I observed that Cherry, his assistant, was flashing him cue cards with words and instructions on them. One said, "Smile." Another said "Say: 'This is Ned Carmichael speaking to you from the Matilda Mountains.'" Other cards instructed him to get upset and so on.

"This is where people come to enjoy a beautiful quiet landscape, but now it is no-man's land," he continued in his melodramatic manner. The cue card said to point it out, so Carmichael made a wide movement with his hand—the camera followed his hand to show what he was pointing at. "Hiking trails, now mined, each careless step can result in a sudden death. Barbed wire and heavy artillery block the approaches to the hill. And the strategic road below us"—the camera showed Lovers Lane—"is under heavy fire, cutting this place off from the rest of the world. No reinforcements or supplies can reach here, and the only way out is through the air."

Until now, I hadn't realized our situation was so desperate, and it was getting worse as he continued to describe it. Everything he described came to pass. However, no matter how intense he made it—heavy artillery, barbed wire, miens, etc.—the insects remained unaffected by the battle.

"Here is Colonel Dan, the battalion commander." As Carmichael said this, Dan appeared in front of the camera. The unit was no longer a small company on patrol but a battalion holding a strategic mountain pass. Wearing a colonel's uniform, Dan was excited, not so much from his sudden promotion as from having Ned Carmichael—who had interviewed entertainment celebrities, sports stars, and heads of states—interview him.

"Dan just told me that this outpost is surrounded by heavy concentrations of enemy forces."

"That's right. We're surrounded by heavy concentrations of enemy forces."

"And he said that we are under heavy fire."

"That's correct Ned. We're under heavy fire." Dan was thrilled. Not only was he being interviewed by the legendary Carmichael, but he was also on an intimate, first name basis with him. Enemy fire intensified, but he continued, "Our forces have suffered, but enemy losses are also heavy."

After Dan stopped talking the camera suddenly zoomed in on Randy's face. He had been killed in action.

"Now, a word from our sponsor."

During the break, the makeup artist applied white powder to Randy's face to freshen him up and make him look better on camera. Then, she covered the blood stains on the wounded soldiers with artificial blood. Real blood, she explained, doesn't look right on camera; it dries out and fades. The artificial blood remains crimson red and looks fresh forever. It never needs replacement.

"Can you do something about his smile?" The cameraman didn't like the smile on Randy's face. He didn't think it was appropriate for a dead man to smile at a time like this. But no matter what she tried, she couldn't eliminate it.

I hadn't seen Randy get killed. It must have happened soon after the battle resumed. The last time I saw him he was crying, wanting to go home. Now, he had suddenly matured, aged by the battle and its flow of time. I stood next to him, feeling the anguish of his death. I was running out of friends.

"Here solder, use this." One of the television crew gave me a can of insect repellent spray. There were flies gathering on Randy.

"No," I said.

"Why not, soldier?"

"Randy is allergic to this stuff."

"But he's dead."

"Doesn't matter. I can't use it."

"This is an order."

"I refuse. He was also an environmental activist."

"What the hell does that have to do with it?"

"He was a member of the Save the Ozone Society. The propellant in this can is harmful to the ozone layer. You know, the greenhouse effect, the warming of the world's atmosphere, skin cancer, and all that."

"A little more won't do any harm. You just go ahead and get rid of the flies. They won't look good to his folks back home." He was losing patience with me.

I began waving my hands to scare the flies away, but they kept coming back.

"Hold the can so we can see the label," the cameraman told me. This was another commercial—Bugoff Inc. was sponsoring the news show. When the viewers see that even soldiers at the front lines use Bugoff, they will be convinced this is the superior product. The camera recorded my futile efforts to scare the flies away. This was how I got a spot on the show.

"That's not the way," said the narrator, "only Bugoff will solve your bug problems." In the next segment, I was spraying the repellent, and the flies were dying by the dozens.

"What a lucky son of a bitch," I heard one of my remaining friends say, but he didn't mean me. He meant Randy, who was now the center of the show.

"This is Private First Class Randy Priday." Carmichael was at his best, covering one of the greatest scoops of his career. "We are bringing you a live interview with him."

Had I not seen it, I wouldn't have believed it. At first I thought there was a prerecorded interview, but no, this was live!

I still had the Bug-off can in my hand when everyone gathered around us. The camera has a power over people and makes them act silly. Everyone was waving their hands or making faces to draw attention whenever the camera was pointing in their direction, but Randy, who was the center of attention, didn't need to do anything.

"And heeere is Raaandy." No one mentioned how odd it was to have an interview with a dead person. To them, the presence of Carmichael was more astonishing than this interview. I was still skeptical, expecting an actor to take Randy's place and speak for him. I didn't remember Randy ever saying anything memorable.

Randy blinked a few times, squinted his eyes, and tilted his head to the side. The place he came from must have been dark, and it took him some time to get used to the light. He seemed confused at first. One moment he closed his eyes, as if to blink, and when he opened them thirty minutes had passed and he was lying on the ground with everyone gathered around him. He was unaware of the time gap. At first, he didn't seem to recognize us, and the smile the makeup woman tried so hard to remove turned into a nervous twitch. Randy's face remained pale. I couldn't see if his natural color had returned under the white makeup.

There were more surprises to come.

"Private First Class Randy Priday is related to Corporal Thomas William Priday, the first British soldier killed in the Second World War," said Carmichael. What sensational trivia this was! In all the years that Randy was my friend, he had never mentioned this, and I doubted it was true. But now, simply by stating this, Carmichael made it true. It wouldn't have surprised me if Thomas William Priday himself came forward to say how proud he was of Randy, his distant cousin.

Randy began mumbling incoherently. I heard him say "flower," "my flower," and "destiny." I attributed his incoherence to something that happened to him during the thirty minutes he was dead. Slowly, he returned to his senses and saw the camera directed at him. A wide smile spread on his face.

"Ned Carmichael! Nice day, isn't it?"

What a banal thing to say. A dull person will remain dull, even if he has come back from the dead, and Randy's case just proved this. Maybe he was enlightened and had witnessed some unknown secrets, or had glimpsed universal mysteries, or had received a revelation of some kind? But Carmichael didn't pursue the metaphysical aspects of Randy's return. He asked more mundane questions.

"Tell us, Randy, where are you from?"

"From Monkey's Eyebrow," Randy said casually, as if the place was well known. I knew better.

Randy's death had made him a celebrity, and I found myself among those who were envious of him, even though I knew I had no reason to be. Randy didn't deserve such a break. He was just lucky to be killed at the right time and in the right place.

Carmichael made further introductory remarks, reading the cue cards flashed at him—words like "heroism," "patriotism," "honor," and "freedom" appeared several times. Carmichael was enunciating his words with a deep, persuasive voice. In front of my eyes, Randy became a national hero. And all he did was get himself killed.

"Do you want to say something to your folks back home?"

"They don't watch the news."

"Don't worry, we'll let them know."

"And Debbie too?" Randy had a crush on her but never had the guts to ask her out.

"Her too."

"Ok . . . Hi, Mom. Hi, Dad. Hi, Bill. Hi, little Sue. Hi, Debbie. I love y'all. I'm fine. I was killed some time ago, but there's nothing to worry about now. I'm fine, really. The army takes good care of us. It's quiet and peaceful here now. Soon, you'll get a letter from the army telling you all about it. I want Debbie to have my purple heart, for keeps. I feel fine, really. Mom, don't worry, the food here is just fine . . . not as good as yours though. And the weather is great. And Mom, don't send me cookies no more.

"You want to know where we are? I don't know myself. It is some hill without a name, only a number . . . 537 I think, or something like that. Can you imagine? None of the hills around us have names either. Dan, our commander . . . you remember Dan, his father sold us that car, anyway, he orders us to shoot at hill 531 or maybe it was hill 547, but I never saw anyone to shoot at.

"Well, at first it was fine. It was a nice day. No one expected anything to happen. It was like a picnic, with flowers, butterflies, and all that. Dan says this hill is important, strategic or something . . .

"Everyone laughed when I told them I'm from Monkey's Eyebrow. Saying silly things about it, like it's a town where everyone is a monkey's uncle. But they're just kidding, like when they say we're the descendants of monkeys . . .

"They scared the shit out of me when they began shooting. That was what Joe and I were doing when it started. Minding our own business, irrigating and fertilizing the ground. Ha, ha . . . now Joe's dead, too. It was really embarrassing, being exposed like that and all. They caught Joe and me with our pants down, if you know what I mean. We had needed relief for a long time. Mom, I wasn't drinking beer or anything. Honest, as I promised you. The army wouldn't allow us to have it anyway. They want us sober. I wouldn't even mention this if it wasn't for the flower."

I moved closer. I was eager to hear about it. Maybe he had learned some secrets after all.

"It all came to me in a flash," continued Randy. "What it's all about. How all of human history, with all its wars, worked toward one end, to bring me here and give life to the flower. I came to this God-forsaken place to irrigate and fertilize the flower. This was my destiny: to help it live. After that, I was no longer needed. I was discarded. This was God's plan. For He provides for all His creatures and works in many mysterious ways, and I was His instrument."

I was disappointed. I expected a more profound truth or a greater revelation. This might be Randy's only accomplishment in life, but having all human history work to have him do this sounded too absurd.

"But I should have known this long ago," Randy went on. "Remember the oracle, the fortune cookie I got at the Chinese restaurant on my sixteenth birthday? It said, 'blooming flower brings much joy.' I still keep it in my wallet. Now I know what it means. Come to think about it, had I known its meaning before, I could've come here on my own, maybe as a tourist, and fulfilled my destiny. Maybe then I could've prevented this bloody fucking war.

"I'm sorry, I know I'm not supposed to use swear words on television, but I couldn't help it. You can replace it later with a gong. It will come out like this: gong gong war. All wars are gong.

"I wish I knew who the gong enemy is. The Matilda Mountains? Where the gong are they? I've never heard of them. It must be some important place, strategic or something. Otherwise, what the gong are we doing here? But this is where my flower grows."

"Cut," Carmichael shouted, ending Randy's litany of words. It was time for another commercial break. "Will you die for us again?" Carmichael asked Randy.

"Why?"

"For the camera."

"I'd be glad to."

On a hill across the valley a human finger squeezed the trigger of a rifle. The bullet spun through the air, leaving a turbulent path behind it, and the sound of the shot followed. Randy raised his head to look around, and he saw the beautiful tranquil hills and the dark shadows of the valleys below.

"Here it comes," Dan said as he observed the shooter through his binoculars.

The camera was rolling fast to slow the motion down for the viewers. The bullet pierced Randy's forehead, and a mark appeared there. He didn't bleed, because he was already dead, and the dead don't bleed.

When it was all over, everyone returned to the place on the hill where he died. I picked up a discarded cue card that had "Smile. Say: 'Have a nice day.'" written on it. I asked Cherry to have Carmichael autograph it for me so I could add it to my time capsule collection.

CHAPTER 10

Outside the television, nothing is permanent; everything comes to an end. This is the fundamental rule of determinism: One thing results from another, and an end follows a beginning. Outside, all ends are permanent; it is only inside that everything is reversible. Inside the television, ends can be changed or repeated.

I keep crossing into the television and into the recorded world, where everything can be edited and played back. Things there can end at the beginning or start at the end. If only I could edit the world outside the television, maybe then my mother would still be alive, as it should have been. But with such editing, I'd have to edit out my stepmother. She and my mother couldn't exist together in the same script. It would be a painful choice for me to make. Maybe it's better not to interfere with the course of events. Some choices are impossible to make. Maybe it's better to leave things to destiny, to their haphazard course, or to God's plan—to something impersonal that makes choices without emotional involvement. I didn't wish to bear such responsibilities.

***

The more time I spent in Our Lady of Mercy, the more I started to worry that someone—most likely Dr. Green—would take the Holy Grail and the items for the time capsule from me. I decided to wrap them in clothes and old newspapers and place them in my small suitcase. I could carry this around with me during the day, and I could also bring it with me to the other side. They were upset about this, not because I carried it but because of the unexpected change in my behavior. What bothered them was that they couldn't explain this based on their theories. They couldn't deal with the unexpected—even in madness, they expect some method. Unexpected and unexplained changes point to shortcomings in their theories; in their world, everything must be explained and have a reason. It forced them to reevaluate my condition after they were certain they had made the right diagnosis—identifying the causes and onset, the prognosis, and the course of treatment. All their neat reports proved worthless, and now they must revise them.

"Why do you have to carry this with you?" Pam ask me. She was even more upset during this visit.

"I must be ready to leave at any moment," I replied. I never told her about the other side of the television screen. "I simply must have these things with me."

"You don't plan to leave, do you?" Until now I had been certain she wanted me to leave as soon as possible.

"Not yet, it's too early," I assured her.

"But isn't it time to return the cup?" By asking this seemingly "innocent" question Pam betrayed herself. I knew that she now sided with Dr. Green and Nancy.

"I'll do it when the time comes." I was deliberately vague.

"And when will that be?"

"I don't know. Don't worry, I'll be home soon, but I must find a safe place for the time capsule first."

"The Met is as safe a place as any."

"They let me take it, didn't they? Safe place, indeed."

As long as I have the status of patient, no one would dare take it away from me. In spite of all their talk, they're trying to spare me another separation trauma.

That night I went back inside the television, but this time, I took the Holy Grail and the items for the time capsule with me.

I tried to find the channel I had stepped into the night before, but the entire scene seemed as if it had never existed. There were many other places that looked similar, but I decided to take my time and try to find the exact location. After a long search, I was still unable to find the exact place, so I settled on one of the places that somewhat resembled the hill. The instant I arrived I knew it was a grave mistake.

This hill and the forest around it were devastated. Only a few tree stumps remained, and their amputated limbs pointed upward, piercing the sky. The stench of death was everywhere. The hill was dimpled with shell craters. Only a large old tree at the top of the hill had escaped unscathed. By some miracle it had survived and was not affected by any of this.

I finally spotted a group of soldiers standing idly by the tree. Their faces were pale, and their beards were caked with dried mud. Their eye gazed forward with empty looks, seeing nothing, and they didn't blink. None of them spoke.

"Hi," I said, "How's it going? . . . Why don't you answer me? . . . Any of you? . . . I'm Noah Miller. What the hell is the matter with you all?" No matter what I said, no one even so much as turned his head toward me or acknowledged me in any way. To them, I simply didn't exist. It was like being in a different dimension—in the world of the insects, a parallel existence that didn't affect these men.

True, I didn't look like them. I was wearing blue jeans, a white shirt, and sneakers—and carrying a suitcase. What was more striking was that I was clean. Their clothes were covered with a layer of dried mud. I was also clean-shaven, with a touch of my aftershave lotion. I could tell from the stench that they hadn't washed for many days.

Beyond the horizon, I saw the flashes of explosions and heard their distant thunder. Occasionally, shells exploded on the hill or close by. I decided to turn back and leave, but as I turned to go, a sergeant, who I hadn't seen until then, popped out in front of me.

"Who are you, soldier? Fresh meat? Ha!" he barked. "Never mind who you are, just take this shovel and join the rest."

Before I could protest, there was a shovel in my hands, and I was following a group of walking zombies, each one also carrying a shovel. They walked like they were being powered by dying batteries—moving slowly, sparing every last drop of remaining energy, avoiding any unessential use of energy, all nonessential systems shut off. Talking was a nonessential function. Scarce as their energy was, digging into the ground was essential, it was a matter of survival. I was digging along with them, adding more dirt on top of the bunkers, reinforcing them against the incoming shells.

Shells were constantly exploding, but rarely was someone hurt. This warfare was different than before. It was more anonymous. No one paid attention to the shelling. They seemed oblivious to danger and continued to reinforce the bunkers.

Soon, my hands were blistered and caused me pain. Everyone lifted as little as they could get away with, which was very little indeed, because we were all in pain. Compared to them, my batteries were still fully charged, and I had no intention of wasting my energy on this dismal task. This side was no longer full of excitement and adventure. It had changed into an atrocious and terrible place.

I was digging, sweating, and aching, wondering if I had become one of them or if I was still a visitor who could leave at will. My perspiration turned the dirt on my clothes into a layer of mud, and I started to look like them. Maybe the others had also passed through here like me and were also caught in this situation, wondering what they were doing here and how to get out.

It occurred to me that I needed to conserve my energy so I could survive and find my way out. The pain in my hands was real. I could suffer here, which also meant the shell fragments could injure—maybe even kill—me. Bringing the Holy Grail here must have made the rules of this show change. It made everything real and made this side of the screen more substantial than it was before.

"I'm Noah Miller," I informed the sergeant in charge of my group. I wanted to establish some human contact, and the sergeant seemed a reasonable choice.

"Really? How about that fellows, this is Mr. Miller," he said mockingly and then spat out a mouthful of chewing tobacco. They began laughing. This was the first response I got from them. I didn't know if I should welcome it or not.

I lost track of time. We must have been digging for hours. The pain in my hands was overwhelming, but I had to press on and continue digging. I became the pain and was lost in it. Finally, the sergeant ordered us to stop, and I followed them back to their underground quarters. Maybe I had turned into an ant after all—living underground and working all day aboveground—though I didn't feel the ecstasy of life like the ants did. All I wanted was a good night's sleep.

The outside stench of death followed us into the underground quarters and combined with the foul smell of living, sweating bodies. A few gas lamps provided what little light there was, and their black soot rose to the ceiling. The ground was covered in ankle-deep mud, and several bunks were arranged along the walls. They didn't have mattresses or blankets. I picked one and spent a restless night on it; thankful it separated me from the muddy floor and the rats.

My entire body ached when I woke up. I had no idea how much time had passed—I had never spend the night on the other side. A heavy explosion shook the ground, and black dust fell from the ceiling. It occurred to me once again that I could be hurt.

After spending the night down here, I wasn't sure whether it was better to be here or up above. The night didn't bring me any rest, my hands still hurt, but I had managed to keep the suitcase with the time capsule items and Holy Grail with me. Every new explosion shook the ground and sent up more clouds of black dust. I clung to my fears and the pain—as long as I had them both I could maintain my sense of being. To comfort myself, I hugged the suitcase close to my body. If I had some immunity left, it was connected to the Holy Grail.

Soon we were outside digging again. Hours passed, but no one said a word, not even a curse—I felt like uttering one whenever I lifted the shovel. The pain in my hands returned, and the blisters became bloody. I wanted to feel the pain. The others were detached from everything. Nothing existed for them, and thus, nothing mattered. I was the only one who ducked when I heard an incoming shell. They didn't care. They had discovered the secret to surviving in hell.

We were given a break. This time, to my surprise, they turned on me. It was a departure from their usual manner of coping—maybe they still remained human on the inside. Someone grabbed my suitcase and tried to open it.

"What do you have here?"

"Give it back!" I demanded, trying to wrestle my suitcase away from him. Luckily it was locked.

"He wants it back, fellows. Here, catch!"

They formed a circle around me and made me try catch the suitcase as they passed it to each other over my head. The more anxious I became, the more amused they became. Then an alarm sounded, and one of them shoved it back into my hands.

"Here's your stupid suitcase. What do you have in there anyway?" And without waiting for an answer he added, "You better take this helmet."

We were herded toward a cluster of machine guns.

"Do you know how to operate this?" The sergeant asked me, pointing at one of them.

"No."

"Never mind, you better learn quick." He pointed out the trigger, cocking handle, and other mechanisms to me, and that was the extent of my training. "When they come at you, you press the trigger and move the gun from side to side. That's all there is to it," he said and left me there to operate the monstrous machine.

Puck, puck, puck. There was a constant rattle of machine guns on either side of me. I wasn't firing. I didn't belong here and didn't wish to be a part of this. Plus, I still didn't know how to operate the device.

"Shoot, you idiot!" The sergeant barked at me.

"I don't know how."

The sergeant grabbed me by the shoulders and we rushed toward the network of underground tunnels, which was like the underground complex of an ant colony. He threw me to the ground in the commander's underground bunker.

It was Dan! He was a brigadier general now.

"Where did you get those ridiculous clothes?" he asked me after he had dismissed the sergeant. My tension subsided, and I felt safe. He knew I had created this scene because before I could answer he said, "Nice spot you picked for us this time." Paying no attention to my protests, he continued, "never mind, as we know, all wars are rough, some rougher than others."

I suspected there was more to it than this. The wars had advanced Dan from a mere company commander to his present rank. Without them, he would have been a major at best. Wars present opportunities.

"I should court-martial you," he said. Then softly, so just I could hear, he said, "You must leave, the sooner the better."

"What about you?"

"I have to stay, but you don't belong here."

Dan was my friend, and I wanted to tell him about the television and how all this was due to the Holy Grail. But I couldn't tell him any of this.

Several strong explosions shook the bunker.

"I didn't expect them to reach us so soon," he said.

"Those men out there are true heroes. I saw them working and not even blinking at incoming shells," I responded.

"Heroes, my foot. Heroism is the stuff of fiction. It's a bunch of scared kids who are afraid to think about what might happen. There aren't any heroes in battle, only survivors. Remember how once, when I sprained my ankle, you carried me from the corner of Lovers Lane all the way to the big rock at . . ." Dan trailed off.

I remembered nothing of the kind and was about to tell him, but then I realized he was describing a safe path out of here. He couldn't give me this information openly. He pointed on the map the exact route we allegedly took; each location was a landmark to help me navigate my way out.

We embraced each other, not knowing if we'd ever meet again, and I left.

He ordered the soldiers to cover my escape by creating a diversion on the other side of the hill. I walked slowly, watching every step, and felt safe following his instructions. When I reached Lovers Lane I turned my head back and saw Dan waving to me. I turned away from the town and followed a section of the road I had never been down before. Farther down the road I made a right turn.

CHAPTER 11

I began walking faster. The stench of the hill followed me for some distance, but I soon started to smell fresh air. There was an explosion, and I saw a large ball of fire rising from the direction I had come. I stopped to look at the spectacular scene. The ball was bright and blinding and swelled to gigantic dimensions. I took the diddle bobbers out of the suitcase and put them on, ready for the cosmic message that might follow the explosion.

When the fireball grew to its full size, a column of smoke rose from its center. It speedily climbed upward, and when it reached its highest point, its tip widened into a giant mushroom-shaped cloud. I knew that no one on the hill could have survived this. In spite of its destructive nature, the mushroom cloud had an immense beauty. It was primitive, cosmic might; the pure energy from which all matter was made—and which existed before anything else. White dust began falling, covering the road with a hot snowy blanket.

The diddle bobbers remained mute.

A few miles further down the road, I came to the edge of a valley surrounded by large sloping hills. The bottom of the valley was flat, oval-shaped, and covered with white sand. I continued to follow the road down into the valley. On the slopes of the surrounding hills, there were parallel lines of rocks, like rows of seats in a stadium. Directly below me—where the slope met the bottom of the valley—there was a makeshift canopy. A man was sitting under the canopy. He was at a table that was covered with various gadgets and stacks of paper. There were also a few empty chairs and mountains of papers all around the table.

The man was busy with the papers in front of him, so I kicked some small pebbles as I walked toward him, hoping he would look up, but he didn't seem to hear me. I cleared my throat; he still didn't respond.

He was short, appeared to be in his late fifties, balding, with graying tufts of hair, and was dressed in a business suit—quite a contrast to the place I had just come from. He was filling in forms with figures, occasionally using a hand-operated calculator—pushing number buttons, cranking a handle to add them up, then copying the sum into his forms.

I cleared my throat again.

"Heard you the first time, dear. You're late, as usual," he said without looking up.

"Excuse me, sir . . ." He looked up, jumped, and nervously tightened his tie.

"I'm terribly sorry, I thought you were my wife," he said and proceeded to examine me closely, tilting his head to look over his bifocals. To my surprise, he got up to embrace me.

"You've finally come. I've been dreaming about this day for years. Please, sit down, and excuse the mess. My accommodations are modest I'm afraid." He almost pushed me into the chair. "May I offer you something to drink or eat?"

Before I could say anything, he poured me some cold coffee out of a thermos and gave me some crackers. I placed them on top of a stack of papers on the table. I didn't know who he thought I was. He examined me closely, too closely for my liking.

"A little bit young, but that'll do . . . anyone will do," he sighed deeply. "Yes, after all these years, anyone will do."

"I'm afraid there's been a mistake."

"No mistake. Finally, a new apprentice is here. Tell me what happened. Did someone goof? Maybe one of the immortals died? Did they open a new world? I was telling my wife, 'Sooner or later they'll make new assignments. They'll have to. New worlds will be created.'" He spoke too fast for me to correct him. "To tell you the truth, I was losing hope myself. But now, all that matters is that you're finally here!" He paused to catch his breath and then continued, "you must excuse me, all these years of waiting have made me so excited, I forgot my manners. Mars," and he extended his hand to me.

"Nice to meet you, Mr. Mars. I'm Noah Miller," I said while shaking his hand.

"Mr. Mars indeed, what a sense of humor." He laughed, but I wasn't aware of saying anything funny. "Good . . . very good . . ." He examined a list on his desk. "Miller, you say? I can't find it here . . . How do you spell it?"

I spelled it for him.

"I don't see any Millers here . . . maybe under Noah? . . . Where are you from? . . . No, nothing here either."

"What' the list?" I managed to ask.

"Never mind the list, it's outdated anyway." He threw it to the ground. "The important thing is that you're here. I'll check later. You wouldn't believe how many pretenders have come over the years. Charlatans, with no qualifications whatsoever. Can you perform miracles?"

"I'm afraid not."

"Are you sure? Any miracle will do. Flying, healing, bringing water out from a rock, walking on water? Anything at all?"

"I told you, I'm not a magician of any kind."

"Magician," he was laughing again, "what a sense of humor you have. Not magic, miracles."

"Mr. Mars, I'm afraid you've made a mistake. I'm not on any of your lists." I didn't know what he was referring to, but I knew I wouldn't qualify. And I didn't wish to be mistaken for one of those pretenders either.

"I don't make mistakes. No one fools me. Tell me, what's your angle?"

"Angle?"

"You know, gimmick, message, or whatever you prefer calling it. Revelation perhaps?"

This conversation was beginning to worry me. He thought I was someone I wasn't and wouldn't accept me telling him otherwise.

"You can trust me to keep a secret. I know all the tricks of the game," he said in a low voice as he came closer—I could smell his body odor—"just don't tell my wife. She can't keep a secret."

If I had a secret of any kind, or an angle, whatever that was, I don't think I'd trust him with it either.

"You're another one of those mysterious ones. The mysterious gods were the most successful. I remember one who was invisible, even to the other gods. There were rumors that he left without completing his work. He did quite a good job, I must admit, and created a lot of jealousy. Yes, and it could work again. But you definitely must have new tricks. People no longer go for old tricks, like burning bushes, talking animals, or water tricks. You must be original. I'm an expert and can help."

"Mr. Mars," I interrupted him, "I don't know who you think I am. I have no idea what you're talking about."

"You're the new apprentice of course. The new god trainee."

"God trainee?" I was puzzled. "Look here, Mr. Mars . . ."

"Wait, who do you think I am?"

"You said you're Mr. Mars." I was uncertain now.

"I should have known it was too good to be true . . . all that mister business. I'm not Mr. Mars, I'm Mars, God of War."

Mars? I couldn't see any resemblance to the muscular Roman god Mars in this middle-aged man.

"Who's your wife?"

"Venus of course."

"And you think I'm one of the gods?"

"God? You? Of course not. Not yet anyway. You're an apprentice god."

"There's been some kind of mistake." His face reflected great disappointment when he heard me say this.

"What a shame. No wonder your name isn't on the list. I saw your antennas and jumped to conclusions. It was my wishful thinking."

"I'm very sorry Mr. . . . I mean Mars. I'll leave now."

"You can stay. At least I'll have someone to talk with, I haven't seen a human for a long time."

Then, he told me about the Academy of the Gods and how Earth—at least the Earth on this side of the television screen—was used as a training world. Before being permanently assigned to other worlds, every new god had to come here to train, practice, and try out their ideas. They came here to acquire the experience needed to reign as a god.

"Some, of course, were more competent than others. A few of them I wouldn't assign to rule over anything."

"Is this the reason Earth has so many conflicting religions?" I asked.

"Yes, but the conflicts are entirely human, not from the gods. They started after all the gods left."

"Left?"

"They received their permanent assignments on other worlds."

"What about this world? Some of them must still be here, maybe to manage the academy?"

"What about it? After they finished, this world was so messed up, no god wanted to stay here. So Earth was left with many religions but no gods."

"But you're here, and Venus." He smiled when I said this.

"We don't count. We're not qualified to rule a world. I'm merely the custodian of the games. They don't come for them anymore," he said, and I detected some bitterness in his voice, "but I know all their tricks. I could help you, and together we could establish something new."

"I've told you, I'm not one of them, and I have no interest in religion."

"How disappointing."

"I'm sorry," I said because I couldn't think of anything else to say.

"So am I. Are you sure you aren't from the arena by chance?"

"No. . ." I felt this was a trap and wasn't sure what the right answer was. "I came by the road," I said, pointing in the direction of Lovers Lane.

"Humans aren't supposed to use that road," he said, "very unusual indeed. But since no god has used it for a long time, I guess no harm was done." His eyes widened suddenly, like he had come up with a great idea. "There was one case . . . someone came as a human and left as a god. He was human . . . but from good parents. Who are your parents?"

"My father is Dr. Miller, a sociology professor, and my mother died when I was a baby."

"Any miracles at your birth?" he asked.

"No," I said as convincingly as I could. I didn't want to mention my ability to see radiation.

"Very unusual. Let's forget about the regulations and other formalities. According to my books, you shouldn't even be here. But you're here, and you're a human."

Of course I was. So far, I saw no divine qualities in him. He looked more like a paper-pushing clerk in a modern office than a god of war. I didn't want to offend him with my skepticism. Maybe he was testing me.

"I see my appearance disappoints you," he said. It was almost as if he read my mind.

"A god's appearance isn't as important as his dogma." I said, trying to lighten his gloomy mood.

"True, very true. But you wouldn't believe what happened to the gods' religions the minute they left." He was changing the subject.

"You mean to say that all religions are false?"

"You better believe it. It was all a colossal façade, a gimmick with nothing behind it. Take this academy, for example, there were no standards, no criteria, everyone who came would pass just for coming, even the most simple-minded gods.

"Officially, the academy is still open, but do you see a god around? I haven't seen one for the last 1,500 years. We also had scores of pretenders and false, malevolent individuals over the years. They pretended to be trainees, or worse, gods in residence, calling themselves by all kinds of titles. We had Sons of Gods, Prophets, Messengers, the One God, and other imaginary titles. Pure fiction, I tell you. There was no limit to their creative imaginations."

"What happened to them?"

"Some were executed. Most were denounced, but some still have quite a few followers. You should have seen the academy in its glory days. What a magnificent place it was at the beginning. Gods by the thousands came here, exchanging and discussing issues, throwing parties, orgies, you name it. Then, new worlds opened and there was a sudden shortage of gods. After that there were no more standards."

"Are the other worlds also human worlds?"

"Heavens no."

"Who made the assignments?"

He looked at me for a while before answering. "I don't know. I asked myself this question many times. The assignments were random, or first to come first to go. What strange religions I saw over the years. One god invented a long list of human pleasures and declared them all sinful, placing humans in constant conflict with their natures and with their consciences. He set matter against spirit and created the body as an enemy of the soul. What a mess. Everything in conflict with everything else. On top of this, he called his brand of religion 'a religion of love.' 'Love thy enemy,' he said. With so many conflicts and antagonisms, there was no one left to love!

"None of the gods made any arrangements for the continuation of their work, leaving their followers in limbo and vulnerable to charlatans. There were those who claimed the gods would return to finish their work and make this a better world. Others said the gods have already returned. What nonsense! None of the gods are coming back. Why should they? Look what a mess this world is in!"

"But you're here, and your wife, why can't the two of you take care of this world? Surely no one would prevent you from doing this."

"I'm the master of the games. That is my assignment, and until this changes, there is nothing else I can do."

"And if you're released from your current duties?"

"Then I'll leave," he said without hesitation. "This world can't be saved by any god. It is too late; therefore, it is better to leave it to its fate. When I was appointed as the master of the games, they promised me it would only be for a few years . . . that was thousands of years ago. The first years weren't too bad. All the gods came here for the games," he told me, his eyes shining. "I can still see thousands of them sitting here and hear them cheering on their favorite team. I was the master of the games. But now," the spark left his eyes, "no one comes anymore."

"And the games?"

"The games must go on. You came at the right time, today is the day. Where is my wife? There is so much work to do, and she is late, as usual."

He was stroking my back as he talked, and this made me feel uneasy. I tried to move away from him, but he kept moving closer to me, and this continued until we both saw a woman approaching.

"You have company, darling?" the woman asked Mars.

She was dressed in a white tennis outfit—shorts, tight shirt, and tennis shoes. I couldn't take my eyes off her. I didn't want to blink, afraid to lose her sight for even an instant.

"Why don't you introduce him, darling?" she said and broke the spell.

"This is Venus, my wife."

"Noah Miller," I said, my voice cracking as if I was a teenager. I felt inadequate standing next to her.

"Nice to meet you, Noah," she said casually, as if this was an everyday occurrence for her. "One of yours?" she asked Mars.

"I'm afraid not," said Mars, "he's more your type."

"Good." Then she turned and told me, "you better watch him, dear, he'll seduce you if you don't watch out." She was examining me closely, slowly licking her lips. Then she turned back to Mars and said, "finally, we have a new apprentice."

"I'm afraid not. He's human."

"Human, how exciting! It's very unusual, you know. You don't intend to keep him for yourself, do you?"

"Of course not."

She began scrutinizing me again, and I felt like an insect under a microscope. It was as if she was undressing me with her eyes.

"Don't let him seduce you." She repeated her warning.

"Seduce?" I pretended not to understand.

"Yes, you know, man seducing man, or rather god seducing man."

"Or goddess seducing man," Mars interjected.

"Nonsense."

"Don't trust her, she is the one who will try to seduce you," Mars told to me.

Mars turned away from me and Venus and climbed up on a chair to try hang a crimson flag from the top of the canopy. The flag had an assortment of religious symbols on it.

"Let me do it," I said. I was taller than him and apparently handier.

"How handy you are. I admire men who can do things with their hands," Venus said to me. She began scrutinizing me for a third time.

None of us spoke after that, and I felt uneasy about her renewed interest in me.

"So," I said, trying to break the tension, "tell me about the games."

The mere mention of the games infused life into Mars, and his eyes shone like he was under a spell.

"The gods stopped coming after there was a big scandal many years ago, although the games are still played on schedule once a year," he began. As he continued, I learned the gods' secrets.

"After all the worlds had received their gods, Earth alone was left without one, but every year, the gods returned to Earth to rest, exchange ideas, and socialize. Being a god is a lonely job, and this was like a vacation for them. The highlight of their annual gathering was the games, which were held in this arena.

"You should have seen the crowds. The hills were packed. Here, behind us, was the grandstand, where the gods from the major worlds sat with their entourages. Some worlds had entire pantheons of gods. I can't begin to describe the pomp and grandeur."

"Those glorious days . . . You had to see them to appreciate the splendor," Venus interjected. She was affected by his enthusiasm, nodding her head as she spoke.

"I'm sorry I'm hundreds of years too late."

Mars pointed to the central section of the arena, which was directly across from us. "Thousands of them, and the noise they made. I couldn't tell them apart, could you darling? And I usually do remember faces."

"Especially male faces," said Venus. I thought I detected some sarcasm in her voice, but Mars paid no attention to her.

"Some of them were strange looking, some were true abominations," he continued, as if she hadn't said a word.

"That didn't seem to bother you, darling," Venus continued, this time including me in her jabs at her husband. "Once, I caught him in the act with that Egyptian one, what was his name? Seth, I believe it was." Mars blushed but otherwise ignored her.

"Some of the gods, some were so strange looking, but as gods they could assume any form they wished."

"Even no form at all?" I offered.

"Yes, we had one like that. We called him the Invisible One. There were rumors he stayed on Earth, and it took many years for us to conclude he was no longer here. No one ever saw him; some even claimed he never existed."

"How do you know he existed?"

"Simple, he was a ventriloquist who could speak from any object. Once, I saw him make an ass talk; he could even make rocks talk. If you ask me, it was all cheap tricks, and when no one had heard from him for a long time, they assumed he left without saying a word. He attended the games a few times, but since then, there has been no evidence of his whereabouts. What do you think, dear?"

"I think he left. He never had any fun anyway. He never enjoyed anything, not even sex," Venus responded.

Mars proceeded to tell me more about the games.

"For centuries everything went smoothly. What a fine job I did, and with no one to help me."

Venus gave him a chilling look.

"Venus helped me . . . some . . . just kidding, I couldn't have done it without you," Mars said, looking directly at her. Then he turned to me and continued, "they expected me to do everything,

149

and with limited supernatural powers. I was lucky that human nature helped me some."

"A lot, darling." Venus's tone still sounded cool.

"Yes . . . a lot . . . they didn't need much encouragement to play. Come to think about it, it was a miracle that I put the games on year after year. Then the scandal broke out, and everything went to pieces. Who did they blame? Me! As if it was my fault that some of the gods began cheating and interfering with the games. All this was because of their betting system. There, behind that hill were the betting booths."

After he pointed out the place behind one of the hills, he put his hand on my left thigh and Venus put hers on my right, each claiming a part of me. I had no place to go, and even if I had, I wouldn't have dared to move.

"It all started with rumors. At first, I paid no attention to them, there were always rumors circulating among the gods, especially during the games. It never occurred to me that they would cheat. It got so bad, they even began interfering with the results, and the rules clearly prohibited any interference. It was pure greed I tell you. They provided new weapons to the side they bet on."

"Weapons? The games were played with real weapons!?" I was becoming uneasy.

"Some could wipe out an entire army at the beginning of the games. And who would bet money if this was allowed to happen? One year, the games lasted less than five minutes. Some gods made a killing that year. Without honest and impartial rules, no one was interested in betting after that.

"Needless to say, the gods stopped coming. Minor interference was always tolerated, but when some of them overdid it, that signaled the end. 'What's the big deal, I said, 'let one god give his side a secret weapon and let the others counter it with secret weapons of their own, that way no side gets an advantage.' But the games had received a bad name." Mars's eyes were wet, as if he was about to cry. "However, they continue, and they will continue until I get instructions to stop. At least now they are as clean and honest as they can be. There are no gods to interfere with them—and no gods to watch them."

"Maybe they'll come back one day, darling," Venus said. Her eyes also appeared to be glistening.

Venus began to stare at me with her blue eyes. A minute ago, I was ready to swear her eyes were brown. Pam had blue eyes, and I missed her very much. Now that I was involved with the gods, I was no longer certain how this would end and if I would ever see Pam again.

"Come, I'll show you around," said Venus. There was still some time left before the games were scheduled to start.

"There's nothing there but ruins," Mars protested.

I still wasn't sure which one I should align myself with. Too much trouble had befallen the world because of wrong choices. If I went with her, I'd be siding with her, but he might be the more powerful of the two. Before I could make up my mind one way or the other, she grabbed my hand.

"You don't mind, darling. I'll bring him back when the games start. I'll bring him back in one piece, I promise," Venus said as she dragged me along with her.

"You better watch out, she'll seduce you," he warned again.

"I'm so excited, I haven't had human company for ages," she said to me when we were alone.

The arena was about the length of three football fields and covered with white sand, which was so bright it hurt my eyes. The sand had been freshly raked in straight lines and was ready for the games, like a coliseum waiting for the gladiators. On the hills around it were the stands where the gods once sat, or rather what remained of them. The marble seats were now broken and partially buried under vegetation. The marble had been engraved, but now much of it had worn off or had broken into pieces, and its luster was gone, even the red rubies and other precious stones that were lying on the ground had lost their shine. I picked up some of them and placed them inside my suitcase.

"I never could understand the human infatuation with such worthless minerals," said Venus. My face turned red, and I was about to put them back when she added, "take as many as you want. There are plenty. Come, I'll show you where the patron of the games sat."

"Mars's seat?"

"No, he never had the honor of being the patron of the games. Mars wasn't important enough for those snobs. Every year they picked one of the important gods to preside over the games. Poor Mars." This was the first time she showed any sympathy toward him. "He was never good enough for them. I tried talking them into appointing him many times, but they wouldn't listen, even to me. He had such difficulty dealing with the rejection. Now that none of them come, he can preside over the games as much as he wants. Poor Mars," she couldn't pass up an opportunity to make a jab at him, "he was only good enough to do the work and take the blame when things went wrong. If you had been a god, you could have been this year's patron. I'm sure Mars wouldn't have minded."

Venus climbed the stairs leading to the patron's seat and sat on the throne. I followed her.

The throne was on an elevated platform, and on all four sides there were nine steps leading up to it. On almost every step magnificent reliefs were engraved in the stone, and they depicted creatures from different worlds. On the highest step, the ninth, there were different kinds of insects. On the step below were mammals, many strange to this world, and human figures were also scattered among them. Then there were reptiles, dinosaurs, and other creatures who dominated other worlds. Below this were amphibians, among which I recognized giant frogs, salamanders, and others. On the fifth step, there were sea creatures, sharks, and monsters of days past, as well as those that dominated other worlds. Then, there were ammonites and trilobites, which once populated Earth and now thrive elsewhere. Following this were images of spices that were successful on Earth and then planted on other worlds. On the second step, there were all kinds of trees and flowers. The lowest step, which was closest to my feet, carried no engravings.

On the elevated platform, there were four sphinxes, one at each corner. They were facing the throne, which sat in the center of the platform, and their right legs were raised in homage. The throne was made of black marble, studded with precious stones, and creatures were engraved on each of its legs. They had a human form, each with four faces turned outward from the four corners of the throne. Two of these faces were beautiful, and two were repulsive. Each creature had four wings, two covering their bodies and two spread out, reaching toward the others. Their two legs were straight, like human legs, and their feet were like the hooves of a bull. Their eyes were red rubies, and they had four human arms.

Venus sat on the throne and invited me to sit with her, but I couldn't move.

"Don't be afraid, come."

I was frozen in place.

"Come here, dear," she said again. But the sound of trumpets coming from the arena prevent me from joining her. The games were about to start.

Venus had her hand around my shoulder when we returned to Mars. I thought about putting my hand around her waist, but I couldn't muster the courage.

"Did she seduce you?"

As soon as Mars asked this, I moved away from her. She hadn't, but I did enjoy her touch and the warmth of her body close to mine.

"Don't be obnoxious, darling," Venus replied. "You and all your young men in the arena." She turned to me and continued, "the times I caught him with that Egyptian Seth . . . and the times when he posed nude for human artists. Do you know what they made him look like? A Super God! They gave him a muscular body. Just look at this husband of mine. They made him look like . . . *the Master of the*

Universe. And that large sword they painted him with . . . he couldn't even lift it!

"Me, desired by god and mortal alike, and he won't pay any attention to me. Do you know how many times I was invited to sit with the patron of the games?"

His face turned red with anger. She had touched a painful nerve, but before it could go any further, she changed the subject.

"Let's bet on the games."

I still didn't know what the games were actually about, or who was playing.

"I have nothing to bet."

"You have something."

"I have nothing." The time capsule was my only possession, and I didn't want to risk betting the Holy Grail.

"Yes, you have." She looked at me suggestively with her piercing eyes.

"Don't let her tempt you. You'll lose." Mars warned.

"It's a simple bet: Win, and I'm yours. Lose, and you're mine."

"What's the difference?" I asked.

"That doesn't matter."

"You'll lose." Mars warned me again.

"I bet one side wins," I said. I thought this was a certain bet.

"Good. I win if both sides lose."

Mars placed three red metal chairs at the edge of the arena, and we sat, waiting for the games to start. My chair was between them, and Venus moved her chair closer until I felt the warmth of her thigh burning me. Mars turned his head away and folded his hands. For a while, there was an uneasy silence. I was uncertain what to do or say. Venus began to stroke my knee with her hand. The right side of my body felt like it was on fire. Mars put his hand on my other knee and also began stroking it. My only relief was the start of the game.

Mars pulled out his pocket watch, took a deep breath, and three cannons fired from the hills at the far ends of the arena. Then Mars inserted a cassette into a tape player and music filled the arena. Venus dug her fingers into my thigh and didn't let go until the music ended. I heard the sounds of a gathering storm. Immense powers were assembling their strength and celebrating their vigor. Playing in harmony, each contributed its strength to the others, all of them reached a spiritual ecstasy. The entire arena vibrated, and the hills around it echoed and amplified the crushing sound of the music. This must be the sound of the universal energy field, but I heard no message in it. It was a celebration of power. It was a hymn of power content with itself, needing no affirmation or recognition from others.

When the music had reached its full strength, I heard a weak sound of discord. It could hardly be heard. It was as if one of the instruments had erred and played a wrong note but then soon returned to playing in harmony after being overwhelmed by the power of music. Then there was another note of discord. It was more persistent and stronger than the first, resisting the power of the music. As the disturbance continued, more instruments joined it, accumulating power of their own, and this power spread, like a malignancy in a healthy body.

The harmony gave way, slowly yielding to the growing chaos and discord; retreating until it collapsed. Each instrument played according to its own tune, disregarding the rest, but they still played variations on the original theme. Then, silence.

Tears ran down Venus's cheeks. Mars blew his nose.

"I always cry at the end," he said.

CHAPTER 12

Mars inserted another cassette, and the arena was filled with the sounds of a large crowd, as if thousands of gods were waiting impatiently for the games to begin. In the background, I could hear vendors offering their goods. If I closed my eyes, the illusion of a large crowd was complete.

"These seats are hard." I said, so Venus gave me an inflatable air cushion to blow up and sit on. "Can't you just command the chairs to change and be soft?"

"Who do you think we are? Anyway, miracles are only illusions. They can be explained by the laws of nature."

"Aren't the gods above nature?"

"No." Mars knocked on the chair to make his point.

I was disappointed. I had hoped these two could demonstrate their powers and prove themselves to me in some way. I expected them to be able to perform some extraordinary deeds. Even their music was disappointing, relying on a cassette player. What happened to the celestial music, the heavenly spheres, and the choruses of angels?

"I hope it's not too loud for you," Mars said as he turned down the volume.

In my head I began wondering why they needed the sounds of a big crowd in an empty arena. Who were they trying to deceive?

"You must wonder why we have these sound effects. We need them for the players, who wouldn't be motivated to play in front of empty seats."

"Can't they see the empty stadium?"

"Yes, but they believe the gods are invisible, and this simple delusion motivates them to play."

Suddenly the trees on the two hills at the far ends of the arena began to grow until they reached a gigantic size and looked like atomic mushroom clouds. They remained towering above the arena. The hills also came to life, I saw small speckles of matter moving back and forth in a haphazard manner, like red ants emerging from their underground nests. Venus gave me binoculars, and on the hills I could see soldiers dressed in what looked like the red uniforms of the colonial-era British army.

"What do you think, dear?" I didn't know what I was supposed to say, or even what was safe to say.

"She wants you to compliment her for the uniforms. She designed them," Mars said. There was some irony in the manner in which he said it.

The soldiers stood still, and I could see them better. Their red coats had two rows of silver buttons, a row of ribbons, and golden epaulets on their right shoulder. Their hats were triangular, with a large eagle on the front. Even the soldiers' long rifles, bayonets, and swords were richly ornamented. All in all, it was a demonstration of poor taste and vulgarity.

"Magnificent," I said as I watched through the binoculars.

"Liar," Venus said. "Wait until you see the flags and banners I designed. If it was up to him, they'd all be dressed in khakis and fatigues. Can you imagine anything duller?"

Without the binoculars, they looked like solid red squares. They stood motionless, ready to descend into the arena. I read the program: "Nineteenth-Century War Games."

"Why would they agree to do this?" I asked.

"To amuse the gods."

"It's cruel and inhumane."

"It's human nature to fight and be cruel. Humans have been fighting each other since the very beginning and will continue to do so until their end."

"There were reasons for their wars," I said, trying to defend my kind.

"Amusing the gods is just as good a reason."

I couldn't believe they were saying this and wondered what their true nature was. My heart was heavy.

Two riders on white horses entered the arena, one from each side. Their swords were drawn, resting on their shoulders like in a parade. They met in the center of the arena and turned toward us.

I couldn't believe my eyes. One of them was Dan. I waved and called his name, but he didn't respond. The other officer smiled at Venus as they came closer, and she waved to him. Then, Dan asked permission to start the games.

"Permission granted," said Mars. "Gentlemen, start your games!" He saluted them, the officers returned his salute with their swords, and they turned back the way they had come.

The beating of drums reverberated across the sound system and amplified the marching of the human squares as both sides started to descent into the arena. I guessed that there were about seventy men on either side. As if driven by one winding mechanism, their feet rose and fell in unison. Left, right, left, right echoed their boots.

When they reached the bottom of the arena, they abruptly stopped. It was as if their mechanism had died and they were waiting for it to be rewound. They stood in the same position on both sides: four squares of men in the front, and three squares in the back that were positioned between the gaps in the front squares. Dan and the other officer were riding among their ranks and inspecting them.

Everything went quiet. There was anticipation in the air, and then something tickled my ear, and I waved my hand. Venus burst out laughing, she was tickling my ear with a blade of grass. I kept pretending not to know she was the one doing this, and she didn't tire of repeating the action. I pretended I was being annoyed by a stubborn fly. The more I exaggerated my annoyance, the more amused she was. Our game came to an end when the games began.

Explosions raised clouds of dust on both sides. Through my binoculars I saw casualties, but no one seemed to show signs of panic or distress. They calmly closed ranks where a person fell. Had I been there, I would have run for my life.

The explosions were coming in pairs. Symmetry was the principle that controlled the games: Everything that happened on one side happened on the other. Everything on one side must be mirrored on the other.

"Isn't it exciting?" Mars asked. "The contestants are equally matched, and either side can win. The gods who interfered violated this principle. When both sides are equally matched, the implements of war make little difference, what counts is human skill and courage. This is what makes the games so exciting."

Now I knew for certain what the gods took pleasure in.

Boom, boom. The invisible crowd cheered after every explosion. The sounds coming from the tape player were like the canned sound effects on a television show. This reminded me that I was on the other side of the television screen.

The sound system announced that all bets must be made within five minutes, after that the booths would close. The ruins of the betting booths were behind the stands on both sides of the arena.

"There was always a last-minute rush to the booths. Some gods had a hard time making up their minds. What glorious days those were." Mars sighed heavily.

"What do you think about it all, dear?" Venus asked as she put her arm around me.

"Great," I said. These gods insisted on constant gratification and praise; without it, they must have felt insecure and inadequate.

A bugle signaled for the troops to march, and the drums began beating again. The two officers marched in front of their troops with their drawn swords, and the troops followed behind with bayoneted rifles in ready position, like puppets pulled by their strings.

Shells exploded, raising clouds of dust and leaving behind red bundles of human waste that littered the white sand. Mars and Venus began counting these bodies and tallying the results on clipboards; Mars counting the right and Venus the left. From time to time they compared figures.

"The numbers must match," he explained to me. "Accurate counting is the only way we can guarantee a fair game."

The invisible crowd was electrified. I couldn't tell which side was receiving the most support. The cheering seemed to indicate they enjoyed the games regardless of the results.

The program now said "Eighteenth-Century War Games," but only a short time ago it had said they were nineteenth-century games!

"May I have a current program? I don't think mine is the right one."

Mars looked at my copy.

"It's the right one."

Puzzled, I examined the troops through my binoculars and saw that their uniforms were different and their rifles longer than earlier.

"No matter how many times I see the games, I'm always as excited as the first time," exclaimed Venus. She was like a child at the circus. Every move and explosion delighted her.

"Of course you are, dear, seeing all those young men . . ."

"Look who's talking!" Venus said, making a face at Mars.

As the distance between the troops got smaller, the cannon fire became more effective, and more red bundles littered the arena. I continued to watch the slaughter, and the gods who enjoyed it, able to do nothing but nod my head in anguish.

"Wait until the end dear, I have a surprise," Mars told Venus.

"Tell me what it is now. Please," she insisted, "the suspense kills me." Mars didn't budge.

"Let me guess . . . you invited some young men from the arena for a party after."

"You know that's impossible. It's against the rules."

"The hell with the rules." She was upset and pointed at me. "He's from the arena, isn't he?" I was a pawn in their game.

"No darling, he came here by the road."

"Why didn't you say so at the beginning?" Her eyes widened. "How magnificent. You must tell me about it when the games are over."

I was losing my bet. The symmetry of the games was so complete that each side was losing the same number of soldiers. Neither side would win.

"Talking about bets, you still owe me from last year."

"Forget it darling." She put her arm around me again, emphasizing her claim over me, "this human is mine."

"Can't we share him?"

"Forget it."

There was a new drum beat. The troops had changed yet again! I checked the program and examined them closely. Something wasn't right. They were wearing crested metal helmets with curved peaks in front and back, like those of the German imperial army. Their coats had a different design now and were not ornamented. Under their coats they had breastplates, which they didn't have before, and they were armed with heavy muskets. I was certain they had undergone a transformation.

There were no more explosions. Although the cannons continued to hurl heavy balls at the troops, they caused more panic than actual damage and only hurt those they happened to land on. The program now read "Sixteenth-Century War Games." This time I was certain there had been a change.

"You're wrong! Look at the date!" Mars told me when I asked about it again.

"I can read what it says, but it is changing. This isn't what it said before."

Mars and Venus exchanged looks, as if saying *what is wrong with this human, disputing the written word*. Written or not, it had changed, but I couldn't win an argument with the gods.

Throughout this, the crowd continued to roar, and the red bundles began falling closer to us. As the contestants came closer, the horrors could be seen with the naked eye. What a spectacular scene of agony and suffering.

The cannons were no longer firing. Each side was in range of the other's muskets, and they were exchanging volleys of deadly fire. As soon as those in front were hit, those in the back would step forward to take their place.

"Efficiency, my dear, efficiency. The closer they come, the more effective their fire is." The closer they came, the more bodies there were to count.

When I used my binoculars, I could see the beads of sweat on the soldiers' faces and the fear in their eyes. I saw the spasms of pain when they were hit. I saw them clutching their chests where the bullets had hit.

The two gods were busy counting the bodies. The soldiers' cries were muted by the roar of the enthusiastic crowd. As the battle was approaching its climax, the crowd became more agitated. The moans of agony must have been there, even if I didn't hear them. Mars and Venus were too busy to take notice of any of this.

It was an orgy of death and suffering, orchestrated by the commanding officers and performed by the soldiers. When the officers raised the hilts of their swords to their faces, the dwindling squares stopped, and the first row kneeled. Then, the front two rows aimed at the opposite side. When the officers lowered their swords, they fired. Like two swarms of killer bees, the volleys traveled to find human flesh.

The squares advanced, and the soldiers who had just fired, at least those that survived, retreated to the back to reload their guns. More swarms of killer bees appeared. After each swarm, there were fewer soldiers retreating to the back.

Time was moving backward. I reached for my suitcase to check on the Holy Grail and see if it was causing the time changes, but it was cool—no signs of radiation.

"Let me see what you have there," said Mars, eyeing me opening the suitcase and touching the cup.

"This is the Holy Grail." I explained, reluctantly giving it to Mars.

"Holy what? I don't see anything holy about it."

"It was the cup of a god."

"Nonsense."

"I saw it radiate energy and change the world."

"Anything can radiate," he smiled in pity. "The gods drank from many different cups, even Styrofoam cups. If indeed one happened to use this one, why should it be different from any other cup."

"But . . ." I protested.

"Let me see it," Venus said. "If it is real, I'll recognize it."

The uniforms and weapons in the arena began rapidly changing. They were medieval knights in heavy armor, with visors shaped like the snouts of wild boars. They had new weapons, and arrows showered them from above. This was not as effective as the gunfire, giving the gods some respite from counting bodies.

"I provided them with those air conditioning systems," explained Mars, referring to the humps they now carried on their backs, "without them, it would get too hot inside the armor."

The program said they were thirteenth-century knights. The program was getting warm from all the changes, and the information in it was getting jumbled. One page still described troops from the eighteenth century. They were medieval knights on one page and Roman legions on the other.

By now the numbers in the arena had depleted. The remaining troops held their shields over their heads as arrows fell, and it sounded like hail falling on a tin roof. When they finally charged each other, they were Greek hoplites carrying pikes of different lengths.

The games were reaching their climax. The beat of the drums intensified, and the troops were now Sumerians phalanxes. I heard their heavy breathing and saw the perspiration on them. They charged for the kill. When the phalanxes collided, there was a shattering sound, like a giant mirror breaking.

My heart was pounding faster and faster.

The phalanxes lost their structure and became a mob of cavemen wearing bearskins and waving wooden clubs and flint battle-axes. Soon, the flint blades dulled, the wooden clubs broke, and they had no weapons to fight with. Or perhaps this was another change. Now they fought each other with their fists, biting with their teeth. They no longer had uniforms, flags, banners, or other insignia. There were no trumpets or drums either. They were a mob of primitive Neanderthals, hardly human at all; savages who did not resemble the civilization that had appeared in the arena previously.

There was a deep silence. The sound-effects tape had run out, and the battle ended.

I was deeply disillusioned.

"I won," Venus said. She had won, and I had lost. But I didn't know what I had lost. My soul? My freedom? My suitcase?

The Holy Grail? What else could I offer her? I knew I had to escape as soon as possible.

The arena was littered with bodies in uniforms from different time periods—from the bearskins of half-naked savages to the elaborate uniforms of modern soldiers.

Then, from out of nowhere, came the two officers who had come forward at the start of the games—Dan was still alive. Now they were dressed in black tights, like ballet dancers, and were carrying fencing foils.

"What a surprise! You always manage to pull something at the very end, right when you think it is all over." The tights emphasized their manly features, and Venus eagerly devoured the scene with her eyes.

On their chests they had purple hearts, dueling targets. They covered their faces with fencing masks as they drew their foils in salute, like Roman gladiators before their final combat, then they bowed to each other. They crossed foils, retreated a few steps, and began fencing.

The arena was silent except for the sound of their foils. It was a duel to the death. The object was to pierce the target. No other blows counted. They tested their opponent with a few exploratory thrusts and then began dueling with growing daring and speed. They moved gracefully, like performing a well-choreographed ballet. They were perfectly matched. Neither had a trick the other couldn't counter—move by move, strike by strike, step by step. Neither gained any advantage over the other.

I watched helplessly; my friend was involved in this senseless duel. It continued until both targets were pierced at once. They fell in unison.

Mars inserted another tape into the tape player and a waltz began to play.

"Let's dance." he said to Venus.

"What a surprise. I haven't danced for ages." The two began to dance a waltz among the bodies.

CHAPTER 13

Dan's body lay in the arena with the other dead, and Mars and Venus were dancing among them. I didn't try to see if he still was alive, or if I could help him. I couldn't force myself to enter the arena, and I wished to be far away from it as soon as possible. It was an abhorrent scene, watching the gods dancing gaily among the dead. I had lost the bet and knew that whatever Venus had in mind for me would happen as soon as they stop dancing. I knew that whatever it was, it wouldn't be pleasant for me. Gods or not, I wanted nothing to do with them.

I knew this was an opportune time to leave and escape while I still could, but I sat there for a few minutes longer, still trying to get over the shock of the gruesome games. I should have listened to Mars's warnings and not made a bet; however, at the time, I didn't think I had much choice in the matter.

Finally, I was composed enough to get up and leave. I was careful not to draw attention to myself. I pretended to be examining the stadium ruins. I walked slowly, picking up more of the precious stones that were laying around. Occasionally, I stopped to look around and see what they were doing. They were absorbed in their dancing and paid no attention to me. When I got a little farther away, I started to walk faster, still looking back occasionally to see if they had noticed I was missing—they hadn't. I started to run as fast as I could and didn't look back. I didn't stop until I reached Lovers Lane. I was breathing heavily now. I wished I had listened to Pam when she told me I needed to get in shape.

Due to the strange sequence of events in the arena, I'd lost all track of time. I didn't know what hour it was, or even what month. I wasn't even certain about the year. I hoped they would continue dancing long enough to let me get as far away as I could.

I arrived back at the place where I had climbed over to this side, or at least I thought it was the place. There were no signs of the battle or bombing, and the hill was gone. In its place was a shopping center with a parking lot full of cars. I saw cars coming and going along the road leading into the mall, and attendants in gray uniforms directed traffic by pointing red and green umbrellas at them.

I welcomed this place as a sanctuary, a safe place to hide from the gods. I could easily blend into the crowd and hide until it would be safe to leave—maybe by daybreak.

I passed through the revolving door at the entrance. Something was wrong. First of all, there were booths offering free drinks. This was the same drink I heard vendors selling in the tape recordings at the arena. The other omen was the music. It was the same music Mars played in the arena. This couldn't be a coincidence, but I didn't want to leave and wander in the dark. I decided to stay here, even if it was risky. I felt more secure among the people in the shopping center. If this was another one of their tricks, I had no escape and no place to hide from them anyway.

There was another thing that should have indicated danger: The shoppers were all women and children. It occurred to me that they could be the families of the men in the arena. Perhaps they were still unaware of the calamity, unaware that their men were not coming back—I expected the terrible news to break any time and turn the peaceful shopping crowd into a mourning mass. I mingled with the crowd. My only interest was to hide here until morning and then try to go back to my world outside the television.

The spot where I could cross back had been on the hill, and now it must be somewhere in the mall. In the center of the lobby, there was a sculpture of a metal tree and a water fountain. This must be the spot where I could cross back over.

I watched the crowd from the second-floor balcony, where I hid behind a pillar. I had a good view of the entire lobby and was looking for anyone suspicious, anyone in the crowd who could be a god in disguise. When I saw nothing unusual, I relaxed.

The stores began closing and the shoppers were leaving. Soon the lobby was empty. The security guards made their last rounds, checking that the doors were locked. The music also stopped. It was quiet, and I was alone.

I sat on the artificial grass under the metal tree listening to the soothing sound of the falling water. It was quiet and relaxing, and I fell asleep.

I slept for what seemed like a long time. I was dreaming that I was back home. I had just completed my time capsule project and deposited it in some deep, dark cave. I had also lost my radiation sensitivity. Pam was expecting our first child, and we were about to go out for dinner. She was putting on the perfume I liked . . . but unless she changed the fragrance, there was something different about it. I was jolted awake by a voice.

"Hello, dear," said Venus. She was sitting on the bench beside me. "You must excuse me for ignoring you, but Mars is such a good dancer. I love dancing with him. Do you dance? I should have asked." She said no word about my escape. It was as if we were supposed to meet here.

"I don't dance," I lied. I felt helpless and trapped. There was no escape from her. She could find me wherever I hid. My escape could have been her ploy to bring me right where she wanted me, playing with me like a cat with a mouse.

"Where is Mars?" I tried to gain some time and delay the inevitable.

"He left in the blimp, did you see it, dear?

"Why didn't you go with him?"

"I won't fly in that thing. Heights make me dizzy. Besides, I couldn't disappoint you, dear." She sighed and winked. "I asked Mars to stay. I told him that the three of us could share the fun together, but he wouldn't listen. If he can't have you all for himself, he'd rather not have you at all. What do you think about my outfit?" She got up to let me have a better look at her.

Her outfit was a ridiculous combination of mismatched styles and colors. She had on a red Roman toga that was held in place by a large golden button over the left shoulder. On her right shoulder hung a large crocodile-skin purse. In her right hand was a large spear, and in her left hand she carried a large, round shield with the head of Medusa on it. The monster's ruby eyes were staring at me, but they no longer turned those who looked at them into stone. Her crown looked exactly like one I saw at the Met—on it were two horns holding the disk of the sun.

"It's nice," I said without much enthusiasm, and I felt she could see through my lie.

I had no idea what her true powers were. It certainly was to her advantage to conceal them and keep me in suspense. An element of uncertainty always was a major source of the gods' power over humans. The fear of the unknown was an element of their mystique. I once read in a science fiction book that in order to block the mind from being scanned, one could occupy it with trivia thoughts. I began adding and multiplying numbers, then I cluttered my mind with nursery rhymes—*Mary had a little lamb . . . Jack and Jill went up the hill.*

"Will you give me one of your pieces of jewelry?" I asked. "It would be a nice addition to the time capsule."

"Only humans attach value to material objects. This is the reason Mars told you the Holy Grail is a fake and didn't come from the gods."

"Is it a fake?"

"Of course not. Everything comes from the gods."

"If they never appear to them, how do they expect to be recognized? Or even acknowledged to exist?"

"They hold power over the human imagination."

I continued to flood my mind with meaningless phrases—*Miss Peel went down the hill . . . five plus three equals seven.*

"We don't have secrets from each other, do we dear? Why don't you relax? Tension interferes with performance, and we don't want that, do we?"

What performance was she talking about? The gods were always vague about their intentions, but I began to suspect what she had in mind.

"Maybe some coffee will help you relax." She looked around. "Too bad the coffee shop is closed."

I relaxed my mental shield and wondered how something as simple as a locked door could stop a god.

"Oh no, dear, I told you, I'm no magician." She smiled, knowing that now I knew her secret. "But I do have just the right thing to make you feel better." She took out a joint, lit it, and took a long toke before passing it to me. I had never smoked the stuff before and didn't wish to try it now, but how could I refuse a goddess.

The joint's sweet taste spread through me; engulfing me. The lights appeared brighter, and I felt euphoric. I wasn't going anywhere. My shields were relaxed, and I was vulnerable to the seductive goddess.

"See? I told you it would relax you."

I felt like I was a hot air balloon.

"How does a balloon feel?" I asked, and we both laughed.

"This is great. How do you feel?"

"Like a submarine," she said, and we laughed again. All my misgivings about her melted away with the sweet smoke. We took turns, passing the joint back and forth. Each toke made me feel lighter and airborne.

"Do you find me attractive?"

I pretended not to understand what she was asking. She was definitely attractive, but I wasn't attracted to her the same way I was attracted to Pam or other human women.

"As a woman I mean."

"But you're not." I protested. "If I look at the sun, I'll burn." My aphorism flattered her.

"Do you find me attractive, sexually?" She was blunt this time. Then, in a seductive voice she said, "I can be any woman you want me to be."

I didn't want her to be anything, all I wanted was to get away from here.

Without warning, in the blink of an eye, Nancy was standing in front of me. The illusion was so real that in the confusion of the moment I almost said "Hello, Nancy." She laughed at my confusion. Her appearance and voice were a perfect imitation. Even if I entertained some fantasies about her, the real Nancy would never have laughed at me. The influence of the joint must have been stronger than I thought. I had to keep reminding myself who she really was.

Before I had time to contemplate Venus's true nature, another transformation took place. This one was even more astounding than the first—Miss Peel.

"Noah Miller, if I remember it correctly. How is Peggy doing?" Then she winked at me, and the illusion was gone. It was Venus laughing at me now. Teasing must be Venus's true nature.

"If this isn't a miracle," I said, "I don't know what is."

"No miracles, only illusions, dear."

I went along with her deception. I hadn't seen Peggy for a long time. She appeared in front of me, not as I knew her but the way she would look today. She looked like Venus. I wanted to touch her hair and see if it was still just as soft. I wanted to ask her where she had been all these years and why she left so suddenly, but Venus didn't let me ask any questions, maybe because the answers weren't in my mind, and so even she didn't know them.

"Just don't become Pam." I couldn't bear the idea of Venus transforming into her, that would be a violation of my most cherished and private emotions.

"Any woman, dear."

I was now sitting next to an old lady. She was dressed in rags and smelled bad.

"Can you spare a dime, mister?" I handed her a coin I saw on the ground. The receiving hand was not old like the rest of her but young and smooth, like the hand of Venus.

"Thank you kindly." From her sack she took an apple and offered it to me. "Here, take this as a gift for your kindness." She looked famished, like she could use the apple herself.

"Thanks, I don't want it. Where are you from?"

"You know."

"I don't."

"Of course you do. I was a camp lady for the players from the arena."

"Was?"

"I'm old now, but boy did I have good times . . . but that was many years back. Now that the gods no longer come, they only have reruns."

"No," I insisted, "they're real. I saw them play and die today. If you were at the games when the gods still attended, you must be hundreds of years old."

"I am, my dear, I am." Unlike Venus's previous transformations, this one was very convincing, except for the hands.

"How old are you?"

"Let me see, they closed the academy about two thousand years ago, and at that time . . ." As she was talking, her image was fading, like an outer shell melting away, and she was changing back into Venus. She must have relaxed her concentration. She realized what was happening and stopped talking.

"Just don't turn into Pam." I repeated my warning, this time more assertively.

Venus shrugged and smiled mischievously. I preferred her in her original form—how she appeared at the arena, if indeed that was her true appearance. Maybe she borrows her shapes from the minds of those she encounters.

She got up and tossed her spear to one side. It moved through the air in slow motion and turned into a serpent the instant it hit the ground, like the staff of Moses in front of Pharaoh. So much for the non-miracle-working goddess! The serpent crawled to hide in the artificial grass around the metal tree.

She threw away her shield and then undid the button of her toga—smiling and teasing me. The robe slides down, majestically revealing inch after inch of her smooth skin. It hesitated for an instant over the bulge of her breasts and then continued to slide down her heavenly body. Now I saw her flat stomach, her hips, and her bare legs. She was wearing a string bikini and a black belt that held a revolver.

I watched with wide eyes—speechless.

She removed her black belt and was completely unarmed. There was no innocence in her smile now.

"Undress," she said.

I couldn't move. I was paralyzed, frozen by her stunning beauty.

"Undress."

Had Nancy been here, she would have been busy resolving the abundance of Freudian symbols in this Jungian situation—two competing psychiatric theories in one place. The setting was bursting with them. The gods have always been shrouded with symbolism, it is part of their mystique. The spear, for example, could be interpreted as an archetype of the phallus and the shield as a vagina. Why did she carry both? Was this intentional or were they merely objects she used? Did this all carry deep symbolic meaning, or was it tasteless attire to which the vivid human imagination attached symbolic meaning?

The serpent also might not be what it seemed. It could be a symbol of the celestial union of Yin and Yang, the male and female elements of the world from which all life sprang.

I was now participating in something bigger than myself. My mind was merging with the collective mind of humanity. Each mundane and simple appearance had a celestial, cosmic meaning.

Even the metal tree was no longer an imitation of a real tree but was the tree of knowledge—or the tree of life. It was no longer merely "I" who was encountering a deity, conniving as she was, this was a symbolic part of the human quest for the gods.

Venus was the divine mother, the source of life, and the demonic mother who devoured her children. She was both of them and neither of them.

I desired her with all my essence. I became my desire and worshipped her, bowing to her wishes without reservations, surrendering to her whims as men always did. I did all this without questioning and without understanding.

Her beauty was spiritual, transcended her physical being, and was beyond words. The color of her skin was like pure ivory. *Tan safely with Solarcain.* Her hair was silky and bouncy. *Love shampoo makes your hair bounce and soft.* Her breath smelled like a rose. *Rose Bud: The mouthwash that smells good whatever you eat.* Her underarms were dry. *Beat underarm perspiration with the Aphrodite stick.* Her eyes were lined with light blue eyeshadow. *Whisk mascara removes rings from around the eyes.* She was the ultimate beauty advertisement. And I was merely a speck of cosmic dust, a solidified morsel of energy that had been created by the cosmic dance of Shiva.

"Relax." She was closing in on me.

"Undress." When a God commands, man obeys.

But alas, disaster! My jeans got stuck on my shoes, which, in my excitement, I hadn't removed. I was shackled at the ankles. I fell down, my bare behind landing on the artificial grass. Had this not been happening to me, I would have laughed at the hilarious predicament. Venus knelt down to help me remove my shoes. After that, all I could do was raise my legs while she pulled down my jeans.

Her touch was electric, sending pleasure waves over my entire body, and I began breathing heavily.

Should I be grateful for my good fortune? Or will the price of this encounter be terrible?

How should I act? None of the sex manuals even so much as alluded to such an encounter. If I survived this, maybe I should write a new sex manual: How to Do It with the Gods.

"Relax," she repeated and gave me another one of her sweet joints. Its intoxicating influence was immediate. Any misgivings I had disappeared, and the sweet aroma filled my body, reaching every organ and cell. I was in ecstasy, naked before the goddess.

She undid the strings of her bikini. When our bodies met, we melted into each other, and our perspiration fused us together. It was pure sexual passion, beyond any inhibitions and without reservations. It was archaic, primitive pleasure. We were united by a pure sexual energy—we were one with the universal energy field. We flew to great heights, and she was not afraid. We sunk to great depths, and I was not scared.

When I entered her, she moaned with pleasure, and I abandoned myself to the ecstasy of the moment. I was devoid of all thought and oblivious to anything else. We were lost in each other and thrust against each other in the holy rhythm of the cosmic energy field. Each thrust was a climax, a plateau of pleasure. Each thrust was a perfect and complete orgasm. This went beyond any fantasy one could imagine. Nothing afterward could match the pleasure and ecstasy of this moment—this thought almost made me lose my erection.

I abandoned myself to the pleasure of the moment until it felt like I exploded into thousands of specks of gold. She pushed me away from her, and I began falling. I was naked and falling into the void, falling down through clouds of golden specks. When I reached the bottom, I landed with a strong thud and passed out.

CHAPTER 14

Ginger found me naked and curled up on the grounds in front of the television. Black snow was falling on the screen. I was back in my world.

I didn't know how much time had passed here. I pretended not to hear Ginger come in and then rush out to call for help.

"He is back with us . . ."

"What the hell!?"

"Where are his clothes?"

"A complete setback . . ."

"He was doing so well, what a shame . . ."

I was still feeling exhilarated from my experience with Venus, and their words didn't register. I felt too good to let any of this worry me.

"I know you can hear me," Nancy said matter-of-factly as she leaned over me. "You had us worried. You've been unconscious for a long time."

Time? I jumped up into a sitting position. The time capsule! The last time I saw my suitcase was under the metal tree in the mall lobby. It was probably still there.

"What's the matter?" Nancy noticed how pale I was.

"What are you looking for?" This time it was Dr. Green.

I knew I had played myself into his hands. All my caution and cooperation would no longer help me. Nancy had probably told him I claimed to be crossing over to the other side of the television screen. At the moment, I didn't care what would happen. My only concern was the time capsule, not what Dr. Green could do to me.

The minute they left my room, I saw the suitcase resting in the corner of my room. Venus must have thrown it after me. She should have had some courtesy and thrown my clothes after me as well. I'm sure she was sitting somewhere, laughing at my predicament.

I opened the suitcase to inspect its contents. Calamity! The precious stones I had gathered at the arena had turned into pebbles.

I examined the rest of my collection, and it was all there: the green hand, the cue card, the bottle of Bubble Bee Soap Bubble solution, the diddle bobbers, and the Holy Grail. No matter what

Mars said, I still felt the Holy Grail was special, and I placed it on top of the television.

I had no idea what time it was. The commotion around my return indicated I had been "missing" for quite some time. I committed my second grave mistake: I asked what day it was.

"You know this." Nancy was unable to hide her disappointment at my setback and wouldn't tell me the date.

"I told you, I wasn't here, I was on the other side of the television screen for a long time."

Nancy gave me a strange look. The damage had been done. Had I told her that I was driving around town, she would have believed me. Had I lied about my whereabouts, she would have accepted it.

"And what happened to your clothes?"

"I left them in the mall, under the tree in the lobby."

"This was behind the television screen?"

"Yes."

Ginger brought me some clothes, and Nancy went out to talk with Dr. Green. Through the door I could hear them arguing but was unable to hear anything besides a few words, words like shock therapy and hallucination. I was certain that he was insisting I receive shock therapy. Nancy objected meekly and was losing the argument.

"I want to leave." I told her when she came back, but she pretended not to understand what I meant.

"Sure. You can go to the activity hall as soon as you wash and get dressed."

"No, I want out of this place. I want to leave. You can't keep me here against my will," I insisted. "I voluntarily committed myself. I came here by choice."

"You can leave when you are well, you are too si. . . not well enough to leave yet."

"Well or not, it is my right to leave. I came on my own and can leave at any time."

"I'm sorry, but no."

"Wait and see what my attorney says about this."

Nancy left the room in a hurry. There's nothing more persuasive than a threat to take legal action.

Ginger came to take me to the administration section. An attendant in a white uniform followed us until we got to the legal counsel office. The attorney could have been Mars's clone! The attendant remained at the door with folded arms.

"You sign here, here, and here, and everything will be alright."

"My release papers?"

"No. Your consent for treatment."

"I don't consent. I'm leaving."

"Not until Dr. Green releases you. At the moment, he is of the opinion that you are not ready to leave."

"Screw Dr. Green. I'm leaving! This was voluntary hospitalization." I knew what my rights were.

"The condition in which you were found prove that you are a danger to yourself, and possibly to others, and you are unable to take care of yourself. Sign this, and in a few days, everything will be okay." He pushed the forms toward me.

"I won't sign anything without consulting my attorney."

"Can't blame you, but we obtained a court order for seventy-two hours confinement for psychiatric observation. You can see your attorney after that."

It was like a bucket of cold water had been poured over me. They could do this if they had a family member's consent. It must have been Pam. She must have signed the papers to have me confined for observation when I disappeared inside the television. I felt betrayed and outraged. However, I still had seventy-two hours before they could start their treatment. I was certain their observations would confirm the need for shock therapy. They had already made up their minds. Unless I could get out of here before the seventy-two hours were up, I was beaten.

Back in my room, another calamity. The Holy Grail and television were gone. I became enraged. I wanted to kill someone and knew exactly who it should be. Dr. Green was responsible for this atrocious deed. I rushed out of my room, shouting and cursing, and headed to his office. I was furious, and for the first time in my life, I became violent. I wished to kill him. I couldn't bear him laying his dirty hands on the Holy Grail.

I burst into his office. He was sitting calmly behind his desk, smoking his pipe. This infuriated me even more. Two attendants were there waiting for me. I was about to jump on him but was restrained by the attendants. I had played myself into his hands. They put me in a straitjacket, led me back to my room, and locked the door behind them. The straitjacket had to stay on until I cooled down. I kicked the door.

"Let me out, you dirty sons of bitches!"

Now I truly was a prisoner, trapped like an animal in a cage. I pretended to calm down, but inside I was just as angry as before. I had to put on this show to convince them to remove the straitjacket. With it on, I had no chance of escaping.

"It's for your own good," Nancy told me.

One hour into my seventy-two hours of observation and I had already given them all the ammunition they needed to keep me here indefinitely and administer whatever treatment they want.

In the evening, Ginger came to help me out of the straitjacket and let me go to the restroom. This was my chance. I made a noise, like I had fallen down, and she rushed into the restroom. I caught her from behind, placed my hand over her mouth, and then gagged her. She was terrified, but I had no alternative. I put her in the straitjacket. By doing this, I sealed my fate. This was the final piece of evidence they needed to prove that I was a danger, not only to myself but also to others. Nothing could save me from the shock therapy if I was caught.

I took Ginger's car keys. There was no one at the door and the corridors were empty. It was easier than I expected. I simply walked through the staff exit. The guard was watching a ballgame. At the desk, I signed Dr. Green's name and asked about the score of the game. He didn't even look at me. I wished him a good night and walked out. As soon as I exited the building I felt a strange sensation and everything went black for a moment. It reminded me of how I felt back in New York City on the subway.

I found Ginger's car and decided to drive to New York City to find the Holy Grail. Somehow, I'd find a way to get it back. First, I would head in the opposite direction in order to confuse them. I used the credit cards I found in Ginger's car at several places along the highway. My trail would turn cold as soon as I left enough signs for them. All I had to do was be careful about not getting caught for some minor traffic violation. Soon every police car would have my picture and Ginger's license plate number.

I left another clue for them to follow. I called Pam, not even attempting to talk under the two minutes needed to retrieve my call.

"It's me, darling."

"Are you alright? We've been worried to death."

"I'm fine. Don't worry, I'll be back soon."

"Where are you?"

"I'll be home soon, I must finish the time capsule first."

"I miss you darling, please go back."

"Miss you too. I'll see you soon."

After this, I stopped at a gas station in a small town on a side road. This was the last sign I left before I headed in the direction of New York City. By the time they picked up my trail, I'd be far away.

I stopped for the night at the Candle Light Lodge. It was on a country road where there was little traffic. I felt it was a safe choice for the night. In the morning, I'd get on the highway. I felt it was safer to travel inconspicuously in the daytime traffic.

"Thank you for staying with us," said the night clerk, not too happy about my late arrival. "You are in room 537."

"Is there another room available?" I thought it was a bad omen. It couldn't be a coincidence. There must be some force of destiny that keeps leading me back to this number. Was there any intrinsic meaning in it? I didn't know. And there was nothing I could do to escape it.

"What's wrong with room 537?"

"I don't like staying on the fifth floor. I'm afraid of heights."

"Don't worry. The room isn't actually on the fifth floor. The management assigned these numbers to give the impression that this is a large hotel. Your room is actually on the first floor."

Indeed, it was a plain motel room: two double beds, a dresser with a Gideon's Bible, and a bathroom. I fell asleep almost immediately.

In my dreams, I saw a thick dust cloud growing until it engulfed me, and I could see nothing around me but its golden haze. It entered me and filled me with ecstasy, and it remained inside me until morning.

In the morning, I shaved and had a hot bath. Then, I went to the restaurant in the lobby to have a late breakfast. To my great surprise, the place was full. What I thought was a quiet, secluded place, was packed with people. Maybe I was too tired last night to notice this, and now I also noticed an Omega Corporation insignia hanging behind the reception desk. This must be one of Omega's holdings. This gave me an eerie feeling.

The hostess asked if I minded sharing a table, otherwise it would be a long wait. I did mind but said I didn't. My tablemate was away when I sat down, but there was a purse on the chair opposite me.

"Hello there."

Out of all the people in the world, it was her! I was in shock.

It was Peggy.

She smiled and sat down. I had no doubt it was her. She had the same wide mouth, the same hair color, although it was in a thick braid, different from the two braids she had at school. She was the same Peggy, only older.

"Aren't you glad to see me?"

"Of course I'm glad," I somehow managed to say. "Where have you been all these years?" For all I knew, she had died a long time ago—being an experimental girl didn't guarantee longevity. "Are you really Peggy?" She could be another of Venus's disguises.

"Don't you recognize me?" She sounded hurt.

"Of course, I do. I'm just in shock . . . after all these years . . . and confused."

"Well, here I am. When the night clerk told me you checked in, I asked the restaurant hostess to sit us together."

"Are you Venus?" I asked. Deep inside I had doubts it was really her. The television world could have spilled over to this side of the screen, and I could be seeing Venus disguised as Peggy.

"Venus? What a silly idea. I'm a tour guide at Omega Cave."

I gave her a puzzled look.

"You came for the tour, didn't you?"

"No, I'm on my way to New York City. I stopped here for the night and will leave soon. I have a long drive ahead of me."

"You must take the tour. A few hours won't make a difference."

Maybe this was a good omen after all. The caves could be a good place for the time capsule. I could hide it there and come later to add the Holy Grail. It would be easier for me to move around without the suitcase, and I also wanted to find out more about Peggy.

She rode with me in Ginger's car. The cave was only a short distance away, but the traffic was all headed in the same direction. We were caught in heavy traffic, and even if I wanted to turn back, I couldn't. The cars were moving slowly, but at least I could take this time to find out about Peggy—she remained evasive.

"What have you been doing all these years?"

"Nothing special, a little of this and that. Nothing important really. What about you?" she asked. "You haven't told me anything about yourself."

"I wasn't the one to leave suddenly to become an experimental person."

"Oh that. There was nothing to it," she said, but provided no further details or information.

"What about all those new and improved organs they were supposed to fit you with? Are they truly as good as they claim?"

"Some of them are better than others."

"Who the hell are you?" I couldn't contain myself any longer.

"No need to get upset. You know the answer."

Did I?

The traffic finally carried us to the caves. I took a parking ticket from the automatic dispenser and the wooden arm of the gate rose to let me in.

"I'll meet you behind the box office. I must arrange for the day off so I can give you a red-carpet tour." Before I could say anything she hurried away.

The parking attendants were dressed in white tuxedos, with red flowers in their lapels, and white top hats. They had assault rifles strapped across their shoulders, and under their tuxedo jackets were red bulletproof vests. They directed the traffic using red and green umbrellas.

The parking lot was four rows long, and traffic was directed into one row at a time. As soon as the rows were full, a large bulldozer came and pushed the cars to the edge of the lot where there was a giant car crusher that pressed them into bundles of twisted metal. The sounds coming from the bulldozer became louder when it flexed its metal jaws to grab its prey. This monster's metal muscles rubbed against each other, making a high-pitched metallic squeak, almost sounding like a metal caterpillar. It was operated by remote control, receiving signals through a pair of antennas.

I was certain the television world had taken over. Maybe it was in control all along, and the Holy Grail had nothing to do with the transformations I saw. Maybe it was merely a tool of the television world.

I went to join the line in front of the box office, where Peggy was already waiting for me.

"Watch your suitcase," she warned, "it could be stolen in the dark. If you drop it, it will be lost forever. We'll find a safe place for it inside." She couldn't possibly know about the time capsule and the contents of the suitcase. I held it tight.

Peggy led me into a large hall and through a door on the left side of the hall. The room we entered was hot and damp. The entire place smelled like human sweat. There were four long rows of desks, and Peggy led me to one of them. A man was sitting there clipping his nails. There was no chair for me to sit on, and I saw that everyone else in the room was standing. On the desk there were piles of forms. He picked up one of them.

"Sign this," he told me, handing me the form and a pen.

These forms released the management and employees from

responsibility for anything that might happen to me inside the cave or on the premises. I also had to sign that I agreed to obey all the rules, regulations, or other instructions given to me when in the cave. Peggy urged me to sign.

"I must read it first," I insisted. After all, I was responsible for the time capsule. The gibberish made no sense to me.

"It's only a formality. No one reads it," said Peggy. "These are standard forms. There's nothing to it."

"What dangers are there inside?" I asked apprehensively.

"There are none. We've never had a complaint." Peggy insisted on me signing, but her insistence only convinced me to read more carefully.

"You can't refuse to sign. That is the rule," said the attorney.

I signed.

"See? There's nothing to it."

CHAPTER 15

We proceeded to enter the cave through a side door, away from the main entrance. It was like crossing a threshold into an abyss. Darkness spilled out from the cave, and no light could penetrate it. I heard a deep growl coming from below us. A door slammed behind us, and the sound echoed through the cave like thunder.

Until then, I had always felt secure in the dark. I always felt the softness of my mother's body protecting me, shielding me from harm. Even though I never saw her in the dark, no matter how hard I tried, I saw black lights dancing around me, creating enchanting patterns. Often, the blacks lights changed into wonderful colors, and among them were the purples, reds, blues, and other colors of radiation. All of them would dance together. It was like being inside a kaleidoscope. The enchanting patterns lured me to abandon myself to them, to unite with my mother. But my eyes couldn't get used to this darkness. There was no softness in it. I didn't see any colors dancing. I only felt the burden and oppressive gloom of the darkness.

The lights Peggy turned on were too weak to dispel the gloom but enough for me to see. We were in a large underground hall. The floor was littered with boulders that had fallen from the ceiling, and there was a heavy, foul odor in the air. It smelled like rotten eggs.

I had a feeling of impending doom, and I turned to leave before we got any further—never mind Peggy, the tour, or my time capsule. I turned to leave but froze in place. At the door was a mannequin with parts of its body glowing. It looked exactly like the one Peggy and I had made many years ago for the science fair. I couldn't believe my eyes. It *was* the one we had made all those years ago.

"Well, what do you think?"

I was speechless and bewildered. This was impossible.

"How did it get here?"

"They kept it in the school basement and were about to throw it away. I took it and brought it here to remember the good old days."

"What the hell is going on? What is this place?" She looked

surprised that I would ask such questions.

"This is Omega Cave, and you are here for a tour."

"This doesn't explain the mannequin, or how and why you are here after being an experimental girl." I didn't want to add that I presumed she had been dead for many years.

She looked hurt, but I couldn't help it. I had never heard of this place, and I had worked for the Omega Corporation for many years. Peggy remained evasive and didn't provide any answers, which only added to my initial apprehension.

"I'm truly sorry, but I have no time for the tour. Now that I know you work here, I'll come back soon to visit you and take the tour," I said.

"With Pam?" she asked. I hadn't mentioned Pam. How could she possibly know about her?

"Yes, of course."

"I'd like to meet her, but sorry, you can't leave without going through the cave. It's the only way out."

The door had no handle, so I pushed and kicked it, but the door didn't budge.

"The tour will only take three hours."

"Three hours . . ." I looked at my watch. It had stopped. I shook it. It still didn't work, but there was nothing wrong with it.

"No clocks work here," she said and pointed at a large

grandfather clock standing along the rocky wall. "There's nothing wrong with your watch."

The pendulum was swinging back and forth, but the time didn't change, and the quartz digits of my watch continued to show the same hour. There must have been some kind of magnetic field affecting them, but I saw no radiation.

"How do you tell time?"

"Time as you know it has no meaning here. Each location in the cave is in a different time, so time changes simply by moving from one place to another."

"Simple indeed," I said ironically. I couldn't see how moving in space could change time, but then, it was like time inside the television, each program had its own time.

We began descending into the cave. I could see very little, but I continued to feel the slop leading down, away from the surface. As a tourist attraction, this cave had little to offer. A dismal, mammoth-sized cave with no stalactites or stalagmites. The air was dry, and the temperature was rising steadily. The trail was dangerously narrow, and there were no guardrails or ropes to prevent us from falling. The safety inspectors must have overlooked this part of the cave. A misplaced step could end in disaster. Occasionally, our steps loosened rocks, which fell over the side of the trail, and it took a long time for them to reach the bottom. I clung to the walls, watching each of my steps. If I fell down, I would never be found, and the time capsule would be lost forever if it slipped from my hand.

Peggy knew the way very well—she never hesitated. I saw no landmarks to help me find my way should I become separated from her.

"Where are we going?" I asked.

"Down, where all the trails lead," she replied evasively.

"And where is that? It's time you tell me. I'm entitled to some answers."

"The trail leads to the basement of the Academy of the Gods."

I took a deep breath of the cave's bleak air. Once more I was at the mercy of the gods. Their web reached out to me from behind the television screen. The inside of the television had overtaken this world. Mars and Venus could now be on both sides. Maybe this was Venus disguised as Peggy.

"This is their academy?"

"No, this just leads to the basement of the academy."

"Where are the gods?" I already knew the answer but asked anyway.

"The academy was closed thousands of years ago, and the gods have gone." She said nothing about the arena and the games.

"What about Mars and Venus?"

"They are also gone. None of the gods are left, and the cave is now a tourist attraction."

"Who or what are you?"

"I'm Peggy." She ignored the what.

"I don't believe you."

"Would you believe me if I told you I'm Venus?"

"Yes."

"Well, I'm not."

"All I see are black walls and deep pits." I decided to change the subject.

"The exhibits are a little further down."

"What exhibits?"

"The exhibits of the things the gods made before they left: their final projects."

We made a left turn and came to a large dining area with many people sitting and eating.

We took a seat at a table in the restaurant. It was set with china, silverware, crystal glasses, a large vase with fresh roses, and candles, creating an elegant atmosphere.

"May I have the wine list?" I asked our waiter.

All the waiters were dressed in long white gowns and wings, but their wings were all different sizes. The waiters glided across the floor. Their long gowns concealed their feet, and when making small steps, this created an illusion of flotation.

"There is no need for a wine list, sir. We have any wine you desire." He gave me an unsettling, eerie feeling, but I dismissed any apprehensions. So what if the cave is unpleasant, this place was so peaceful and beautiful, there was nothing to justify my suspicious mind.

"Anything?" I asked.

"Absolutely."

"Tirosh 1887. I'll have that."

"Yes, of course." He wrote down my order without blinking an eye. Never mind that I just made it up. I didn't even know if such a wine existed. In this place, anything was possible. Why shouldn't I take advantage of it?

"Excellent choice," he said. Then he leaned toward me and whispered, "most people would go for the 1898 vintage, but the 1887 was far better."

When he brought the bottle, he offered me the cork to smell and had me taste the wine before pouring it into the glasses.

"Excellent bouquet . . . great body . . . but it tastes like . . . I would say early twentieth century, 1914 to be more precise." I was making it all up of course.

"Let me see . . ." the waiter said, visibly turning pale. He tasted the wine. "I'm so sorry, sir. You're right. It is a different vintage. Let me take it back."

I had no idea of course what wine or vintage it was, but it was clear he didn't want to lose face.

"It is such a pleasure to serve someone who understands wines and has such exquisite taste. Most people will drink anything you put in front of them," he told me as he handed the bottle over to another waiter to take it away and bring us the proper bottle.

I still had an unsettling feeling about the place, and then Peggy began talking about the past.

"And don't tell me, Noah Miller, that it was right for the Space Warriors not to accept girls. I could shoot as good as any boy."

"You're absolutely right," I said, but I didn't care one way or another about the decades old policy. My response only encouraged her to continue.

"Girls can do anything boys can."

"I'm sure they can."

"Well . . ."

"Well what? The Space Warriors haven't existed for many years."

"So, admit that it was wrong."

"It was wrong."

She grinned in victory.

The wine and the music began doing their trick. I was getting more relaxed. I saw that somehow everything in the world was coming together and gathering into a single point here in the basement, but a restaurant didn't belong in this dismal cave!

The theme of the restaurant was heaven, and I must admit it was skillfully done. The ceiling was made using blue paneling, which had blinking lights on it arranged in constellations. The space was open, as if it stretched endlessly in every direction, and it was full of people eating under the most wonderful crystal chandeliers I'd ever seen. They were suspended in midair by invisible cables, creating an illusion of floating under the constellations on the ceiling.

"Another of the gods' creations?"

"No, the restaurant was added by the Omega Corporation."

We drank more wine and continued to discuss "the good old days." I wasn't sure if we had actually shared these days together, but we pretended it was all true. I didn't know what her motives were, but I knew mine. I was dependent on her to get out of the cave. Three hours until it is over, she had told me at the beginning. I was certain this place was not what it appeared to be. It wasn't a regular restaurant, and it definitely wasn't heaven. With the television world in control, everything was different. Norms of sanity and insanity were different. And when anything is possible, there is no criteria to distinguish what is normal and what is not. There was no way of telling them apart. The normal and the abnormal—sanity and insanity—could be reversed.

Pam would have loved this place. I missed her, and as soon as I could get out of this place, I'd go back to the institution, subject myself to whatever treatment they decided to give me, and then go back home to Pam and forget about the time capsule and Holy Grail. But first I had to get out of the cave. If the basement really was full of things made by the gods, there could be more surprises.

Several couples danced to the music. I saw that, in addition to a chandelier, every table also had a clock hanging above it, each showing a different time. The clock at our table was set at six forty-six, which was the time Peggy and I met for our first date.

"Remember our first date, when all you could afford was a hamburger. And those four guys who came to meet the clowns and we beat them to win the prize. Remember?" she asked me.

We both laughed.

"Imagine if those four adults had received the diddle bobbers. You kept them for your time capsule, didn't you?"

I didn't remember mentioning the time capsule to her, and definitely not its contents. She looked like Peggy, and she seemed to share some of my childhood memories, but the real Peggy couldn't know about these things—but Venus could.

I wondered what Pam was doing now and how the television

world was affecting her.

"I bet they serve delicious food here," I said.

"Everything here is delicious," she said. She looked like she was about to add something more, but then a man approached our table. "Oh, here is Bob. He can tell you more. He's my supervisor, so ask him anything."

Bob joined us. His nameplate said Robert Virgil. I disliked him immediately. He looked like Dr. Green, that is, if Dr. Green had grown a beard and dressed like a park ranger. Bob also had a tick in his left eye, which Dr. Green didn't have.

"Have we met before?" he asked me.

"I don't think so."

"Do you mind if I smoke?" I did mind, but he didn't wait for permission and lit his pipe.

"What's the shortest way out of here?" I asked him.

"There are no shortcuts, only different ways. You must take the full tour, that is the only way out."

I had dozens of questions about the cave, and Bob proved to be a better source of information than Peggy.

"Didn't Peggy tell you? This is the basement of the Academy of the Gods. The basement was used for storage. It was never really part of the academy."

"Storage for what?"

"The gods' graduation projects. Before receiving their assignment to another world, the gods had to submit a final project. No one could graduate without submitting one."

"Submit to whom?"

"To no one in particular. They just had to do it." The tick in his eye was more pronounced now.

"Someone had to receive the projects, look them over, and evaluate them."

"There was no one to evaluate the gods, and there were no criteria for evaluation. Every project was acceptable."

"What was the point then?"

"It needed to be done and that was that." The harder the question I asked, the more pronounced his tick became. "The purpose of the projects was to ensure the continuity of their doctrines after they left and to keep their followers from drifting away. Without this, there was a real danger of nihilism and anarchy."

"It makes sense to keep summaries of their doctrines in one place," I commented.

Peggy and Bob laughed.

"You mean a library?" Peggy asked.

"Yes."

"All the books were written by humans, not gods. The basement stores a different kind of project . . ."

The conversation was interrupted by a waiter who came to take our order. I asked for a menu, but there were none.

"You can order anything you wish. We have it all," said the waiter.

Peggy ordered bran cereal, and I told Bob to order next. He ordered an exotic meal: stuffed sea horses, bird nest soup, and a Himalayan capon marinated in Slivovitz.

"I'll take the same," I said, not knowing what else to order. But then I had second thoughts. "You said I can have anything I wish?"

"Absolutely."

"I want to have the best dish my mother ever made."

"That will take some time."

"Never mind the time, I'll wait."

"Very well, as you wish, sir." The waiter wrote down my order. I knew I had played myself into their hands. They could bring me just about anything, and since I had never tasted my mother's cooking, I wouldn't be able to tell the difference.

Bob insisted on eating before telling me more about the cave. After his food was served, his full attention was directed to the food and the pleasure of eating. Suddenly, when they were about to serve my dinner, Bob reached for a drink of water and disappeared. He vanished through a trap door that opened under him without warning. The trap door closed immediately after he fell in.

"Where did he go?" I managed to ask.

"He was raptured," said Peggy, calmly stirring her cereal.

Bells and cymbals began to ring, and the angels were applauding and congratulating the two angels who had attended Bob.

"Let's leave."

"You haven't even touched your food," Peggy said.

"Damn the food, look what happened to Bob!"

"Oh, him. You needn't worry. There isn't a trap door under you, you're a guest."

I heard more bells and cymbals and assumed more trap doors were opening under unsuspecting diners. Each time I heard the bells and cymbals, it was like seeing poor Bob again. I watched every step I took and tried to walk behind Peggy, stepping on the same spots.

"I want to see where he fell to."

"There is nothing to see, it's one of the oldest and simplest exhibits. It will only add to your time here."

"Never mind that." Had I not met him, even if briefly, I wouldn't have insisted on this.

"Don't forget your suitcase," Peggy warned. I had almost forgotten about it. Somehow it seemed less important now. Before his fall, Bob had told me that there was nothing in the cave that didn't exist outside. Maybe I was in a giant time capsule made by the gods—the Omega Corporation had beaten me here.

We headed down a spiral staircase under the restaurant. At the bottom there were rows upon rows of large black pots. There was steam coming from them and a foul odor. I must be dead and in hell, on a grand tour before being assigned to one of the pots. Or maybe worse.

Groups of people were wandering around, joking and giggling nervously, banging on the pots, and touching them to check their temperature. I didn't ask what was cooking. Supervising angels with long tridents walked around with somber expressions, occasionally stirring the pots and pushing down round objects that popped up to the surface from time to time.

In spite of the heat, I was covered with cold perspiration. It was my bad luck to come without a camera, without a way of gathering evidence. Maybe it would be better not to have evidence. From time to time, I saw a trap door open and objects I couldn't identify fell into the pots with a splash.

"Is this hell?" I asked Peggy.

"There is no hell. Think of this as like a visit to a theme park."

"Which god graduated with this dismal project then?"

"I can't give out such information."

To leave this place, we had to cross a bridge spanning a pit of fire. It was wide at one end and narrow at the other. At both ends of the bridge there were some broken tridents, which had been used to prod those attempting to cross. I couldn't read the Egyptian hieroglyphs written on a plaque near the bridge, but I got the gist of their meaning.

We passed bins holding toads and serpents that, according to some old and primitive traditions, were fed to the tormented. How inadequate and pathetic my time capsule was, trying to assemble samples of human culture. Such achievements paled in comparison to these implements of destruction and torture. What did I have to offer in my time capsule? Items that were worthless without the Holy Grail.

"There's a better place to dispose of it," Peggy said, seeing me ready to cast the suitcase into the pit.

As we continue to walk through the cave, I witnessed many atrocities and horrors. We walked through hells from many traditions, only a few of which I recognized. All of them were places of suffering and eternal damnation. The suffering was everlasting. It was the domain of the dead, but without death.

"Of course, they all are mannequins. There is no life here. These are exhibits of the gods' final projects and aren't real."

"Mannequins?"

"Of course. The gods weren't as cruel as people imagine."

Indeed, to instill fear in the hearts of humans, just the rumor of this being real was enough. Guide one or two people through this place and then let them return to tell others about it—this was enough for their purposes. But the torments I saw were too believable, and often the mannequins were very human looking.

"What about the angels?" I asked. "Are they real?"

"They're like the rest."

"And you and Bob?"

"We're real."

"Real what?"

She ignored my question.

As we approached the modern section, I saw some blonde-haired maidens bathing in a spring of pure water. They had milky skin, which looked whiter amid their bleak surroundings, and were using bars of soap made from human fat.

I saw no original ideas, and Peggy continued to assert—over and over again—that there was nothing in here that didn't exist outside. The gods incorporated things they had seen into their systems, or maybe human ingenuity had exhausted all possible means of affliction, leaving the gods without any alternative but repetition. On the other hand, maybe they decided to use what was familiar to humans.

I saw angels who were dressed like Catholic priests. They put people—or mannequins—on the rack, stretching them taller. They also screwed their thumbs, introduced them to the Iron Maiden of Nuremberg, and put them to sleep in the Bed of Procrustes. I knew at once that this was not original but copied from the Inquisition.

At the entrance to a pavilion, there were scores of starving children laying on the ground. Their bellies were swollen from hunger, and angels of mercy walked among them to comfort them, patting their heads and kissing them.

After passing this, we came to a bright place, an oasis of light in the midst of the gloom.

"We could have started here, had you not insisted on looking for Bob. There is a direct path to get here from the restaurant," Peggy stated.

This place was illuminated by psychedelic lights, and mirrored globes were rotating above our heads, creating dancing spots of light. There were people wandering around, and among them were clowns performing tricks. Groups of people gathered to watch them. They were handing out balloons and toys to both children and adults. Many of the clowns were wearing diddle bobbers on their heads, and machines were making thousands of soap bubbles that floated in the air, reflecting the light until they burst.

The festive atmosphere cast aside my gloomy mood, and the horrors I had just witnessed no longer seemed real. If Peggy was telling the truth, and it was indeed only mannequins who were being tortured, my sympathy could be misplaced. But Bob was real, and he fell to his fate. Maybe this was the turning point of the tour. I expected everything to become brighter and more cheerful now—perhaps I would see the exhibits of more agreeable gods.

Vendors offered refreshments and snacks, and jugglers were throwing and catching objects to the admiration of a watching crowd. But not all was as it seemed. The janitor clown scowled at me for spilling some of my popcorn. He even pulled out a gun and was ready to shoot me. It didn't matter that I was going to clean it up. I apologized and pleaded for mercy. My heart stopped, and I was ready for the worst. He wouldn't even listen to Peggy. Soon, people gathered around us. None of them intervened on my behalf, and some even encouraged him to shoot me.

To the delight of the crowd, out from his gun came a squirt of water. A supervisor clown came to see what the commotion was and reprimanded him for causing me such embarrassment. The offending clown knelt in front of me to beg my pardon, which I graciously granted. But the supervisor insisted on a proper punishment. The clown presented me his rear end to kick and then farted loudly. The crowd thought this was hilarious. The clown took out the remnants of a busted condom from his pants, and for the first time since I had come to the cave, I laughed.

"Come," said Peggy, pulling me through the crowd and leading me into a large theater with seats arranged around a glass booth. Guards wearing pantaloons with wide red stripes and curved pointed shoes with bells at the tips, and holding large scimitars in their hands, were posted at each corner of the booth.

The place was soon full. The lights went off and spotlights were directed at the booth. Large television screens showing its interior descended from the theater's ceiling.

In came three beautiful women, and the crowd applauded with enthusiasm. The women started to dress, and to my surprise, their breasts were old and shriveled—older than suited their youthful appearances. I felt discomfort at discovering their secret. They lifted the loose skin of their breasts, stuffed them inside plastic implants, and molded them into a youthful shape. They put on their bras, and then makeup and jewelry, and finally, they dressed. Three men came with bouquets of roses. They sat down to chat, eat, and drink. It was a dull show.

They began to make love to the women, and the dull show transformed into an erotic display. They were fondling each other and undressing. The camera showed everything in slow motion so that no detail would be lost. I saw the men's hands moving slowly along the women's tights under their skirts. Soon, they all were naked. Peggy's fingers dug into my arm, but before I could protest in pain, the men reached out to fondle the swollen nipples of the women and there was an explosion inside the booth. The erotic scene came to a gory end. Fondling the nipples had triggered explosives in the breast implants.

On the screens, it was being repeated in slow motion. The plastic implants expanded and became balls of volatile gas that tore apart their skin and shattered their bones. The glass became a canvas, splashed with spots of colors, as if a modern artist was making an artistic statement about our chaotic world.

The crowd was shocked. There was an initial silence, but then everybody started to speak at once, and a few screamed. I was surprised to hear some approve of the terrible deed and applaud.

"Why?" I managed to ask.

"I don't really know," Peggy shrugged, "No one does. The reasons aren't important; it's the deed itself that counts in the eye of the gods."

I got up to leave but Peggy forced me back into my seat.

"The best is yet to come."

A bell gave a signal, and the camera played everything in reverse. Everything undid itself in slow motion. The shattered particles moved away from the glass and reassembled, and all the events reversed themselves, undoing the terrible ending: Body particles moved back to form blood vessels, organs, and limbs; the women's breasts reformed; the men took the flowers they brought and left, walking backward; and finally, the women took out the plastic implants and their breasts were old again.

"See," Peggy said. "I told you this is the best part. Everything is reversible."

But something was wrong. Not all the parts were correctly reassembled. In the booth there were three human monsters; eyes on their buttocks, legs coming out from their heads, and other abnormal combinations of human parts. It was a variation on a theme—modern art in the making.

The temperature was rising, and it became very hot as we left the theater. So hot I was tempted to jump into the pool that appeared in front of me a little further into the cave. Many people were jumping in with all their clothes on, and before I could stop her, Peggy also jumped in.

I was aware of the danger even before we got there. When we got closer, my radiation sensitivity kicked in, and I saw that the pool emitted fatal doses of gamma radiation.

Peggy paid no attention to my warnings and dared me to join her. I moved to a safer distance, but not before she splashed me. Jumping in was like dipping into a purifying ritual pool, which cleansed those who were baptized in it. I saw ironic justice in this. I didn't know whether the dose I received was fatal. I suddenly felt very good all over my body. The radiation I received was fatal to all the microorganisms and parasites living on my body. Even my eyelids were lighter, as the small parasites living there, which resembled miniature dinosaurs, died and evaporated with a hissing sound as soon as they reached the ground. The people in the pool were already dead, but they didn't know it yet.

Should I have warned them?

Peggy came out, dripping with radiation-saturated water, and dried herself. I kept a safe distance from her. The glow on her body ceased when she dried off.

"You must be crazy, swimming in that pool. Do you know what it can do to you?"

"I know."

"Why did you do such a stupid thing?"

"To cool off. I was hot. Don't worry, it won't harm me."

I gave up. She could be right, maybe her replacement parts were not susceptible. And so we continued downward, deeper underground.

We passed a small door, and I heard the most incredible sound. From behind the door, I heard canaries singing.

"I want to go in there," I said, but Peggy tried to discourage me from entering.

"You'll be sorry," she said as I opened the door.

We entered a hall. The walls, ceiling, and floor were all made of mirrors. Even the door was a mirror, and when closed, it blended into the wall and could hardly be seen. There were canaries flying around and singing. It could have been multiple canaries, or a single canary reflected countless times. Some flew toward the mirrors, while others flew backward; some flew to the left, others to the right. They were constantly colliding and falling down.

I couldn't tell how big the place really was. The mirrors stretched into infinity in every direction. And there were singing canaries in all the images. There were also images of a man. He was sitting on a chair made of some invisible substance, like he was suspended in midair. He was twisting and moving in despair, something must have been eating him from the inside.

I couldn't tell if I was next to him or next to one of his images. Peggy and I were holding hands in order to not to get separated and lost among the reflections.

"What's the matter with him?"

"Nothing is the matter with me," said an image beside me. "If only they weren't staring at me."

"It's only your reflection, I told him. "None of them will stare at you if you don't look at them. They do everything you do."

"If only I could get away from them. Even when I close my eyes, I feel their stares. When I open my eyes, there they are again, staring."

"Why don't you just walk away? There is nothing here to hold you. The images won't exist if you aren't here."

"I tried it once. They followed me everywhere. They became invisible. At least I can see them in here and keep an eye on them as they plot against me or jump to attack me from behind. You can never tell what they are up to."

There was something strange about the images. When he spoke, only one of the images talked, the rest were quiet, not moving their lips. They just stared at him and said nothing. Their mouths were half open, but whatever they intended to say remained unspoken. Some pointed fingers at him, others had a loathing expression, and only a few had somewhat more pleasant looks. They all were, without a doubt, a reflection of him, but not an exact one. They were his appearances during different times in his life, and they all were staring at him.

"And what will happen to them without me? They are all mine. I am responsible for them." He spoke as if they were true persons, not merely reflections.

"After they disappear, you'll forget all about them."

"No, I can't let them go. It is my duty to myself. I have to account for all of them and see that none of them go missing."

"I'm truly sorry."

"That's all I get, lots of sympathy. No real help from anyone."

"I'm only a visitor here, and I'm sorry I can't help you."

"That's what they all say."

"We can't stay any longer," said Peggy, elbowing me.

"Why the canaries?" I asked as we were leaving.

"To keep me from falling asleep," he shouted at us. And the charm of the canaries was gone.

"I guess he is better off than those we saw before?" I asked.

"Worse, much worse," said Peggy. "You see, he remembers every moment of his life. He constantly relives them and remembers all his pain, failures, and disappointments. They haunt him and will follow him wherever he goes. Forgetting is the secret of eternity. The only way to survive it without suffering is by forgetting and only living in the moment. This is the gods' secret."

We came to the lowest part of the cave. It was very hot, and the walls were glowing red with heat. The attendants here were naked because of the terrible heat, and a foul smelling substance was bubbling in a pond where all the sewage drained. Peggy told me it was the center of the Earth and the source of energy that runs the cave. I saw no radiation here. After this, our tour can go only upward, closer to the surface.

"This is the place," said Peggy.

"What place?"

"For the time capsule of course."

I opened my suitcase for a last look at the objects I had collected. In a way, I was relieved the Holy Grail was missing. I took out the diddle bobbers and put them on my head. And I also took out the bottle of Bubble Bee Soap Bubble solution and put it in my pocket. Why? I don't know, maybe for sentimental reasons. I swung my arm, tossed the suitcase into the bubbling pond, and then watched as it disappeared.

We crossed a narrow bridge over the foul pond. On the other side, we were greeted by a woman in a white gown.

"Nancy!" I said in surprise, but she only looked like Nancy. I felt at ease. Maybe the worst was over.

There were several wooden chairs with leather straps with buckles attached to them, and she politely asked us to sit down. Two husky attendants appeared from out of nowhere—a hint that we better sit down, or else—and one of the attendants strapped me to the chair. Peggy also was strapped to a chair, but she showed no concern. I was helpless. The woman smiled pleasantly and told me to relax, but I had no reason to relax. They put a helmet with earphones on my head.

"The management is glad you are here and thanks you for

your cooperation in our experiment."

Experiment? What experiment? The word made my heart sink. Could it be an experiment conducted on behalf of the gods? Another of their projects?"

"There are ten buttons to your right. Please try to reach them. If the straps are too tight, we'll be glad to adjust them. The buttons are numbered from one to ten. By pressing the different buttons, you'll control the degree of pain delivered to you."

I wasn't going to press any buttons, and I made a fist in protest.

"Each experience of pain will be followed by a respite period, the length depends on the level of pain you choose. The higher the pain level, the longer the respite period. You must make your choice within five seconds after the red light comes on. The penalty for failing to choose is the eighth level of pain. When the respite period is over you must make another choice. For every choice, you will be rewarded tokens according to your selection. This is our way of thanking you for your cooperation. Thank you and have nice day."

I wanted to shout that I didn't consent to be part of the experiment, but then the red light came on.

"Please make your first choice."

Five, four, three, two . . . I had to make a choice, so I pressed number one, and three tokens rolled into the receptacle.

Nothing happened at first, but then I suddenly felt something. It was like hundreds of needles piercing me at once, puncturing my entire body and slowly reaching every nerve. As soon as the pain reached its highest level, it began to recede, and I expected it to end, but no, there was another burst of pain. I made an effort not to cry out—not wanting to give them the satisfaction of my pain.

The clock was counting down. I felt no pain now, but I'd need to make another choice. I panicked and pressed one again. I expected the pain to come in the same manner as before, but this time it was different. The needles came one by one, attacking different locations one after the other. The first level was intolerable, and the respite period was too short to make up my mind. I needed more time to recuperate my strength.

I selected the sixth level. Tokens rolled into the receptacle, and then I suffered more than I thought I could endure. I suffered spasms and cramps, dull burning needles pierced me, and bullets gnawed and burned inside of me.

After this, I gained fifteen minutes of relief, but another decision was coming. I was twisting restlessly in my seat, but the straps wouldn't loosen. The relief period was too brief for me to recover, and suddenly I felt the pain of the eighth degree.

This pain chewed each of my body's cells. It delivered pain

directly to my brain, inflicting pain in the left half of the brain and triggering all the imaginary pains in the right half. The electrodes delivered a higher voltage, and my body was exploding from the inside out. I needed a full hour of respite, even if trying to get it killed me. I pressed the tenth level. I braced myself for a surge of terrible pain.

I waited.

I pressed the tenth button again. Nothing. I pressed again and again, and no pain was delivered. I looked over and saw that Peggy's chair was empty. I began laughing hysterically. The experiment was over. There was no pain at the tenth level. There was only the fear of it. Was it another of the gods' secrets? The straps came off my hands, and I was free. I learned another of the gods' secrets: After fear is created, there is no need to be cruel.

We continued walking and reached a patch of brick pavement marked with two solid yellow lines. I felt home free; the road was leading upward. There were vending machines selling different kinds of food, and we could use the tokens we had earned to purchase things from them. I had more of them than Peggy, who hit the tenth level right at the start and didn't suffer any pain—she had insider information. I gave Peggy my tokens so she could decide how to spend them. She decided to save them and use them when we got closer to the Other Place. I hoped that it was a place of bliss and beauty.

"Was it also made by the gods?" I asked as we walked.

"There were rumors that it was made by humans."

"It must be nice."

"I don't know. I've never been there."

"Is it outside?"

"No, outside is hell."

"So what is this place?" She didn't answer.

The road led to a small bronze door. Behind this door was the Other Place. Along the wall on either side of this door were more displays, like a carnival midway. Peggy decided to spend our tokens here.

For a few tokens, a group of Hassidic rabbis played football while still dressed in their traditional attire—black gowns, prayer shawls, and wide fur hats.

"Watch out!" I yelled to Peggy as a rabbi carrying the ball rushed toward her. When he was about to collide with her, he passed right through her. I tried to touch them, but my hand met empty space.

They were holographs, three-dimensional illusions the gods made for their private amusement. It was a crude sense of humor, but I welcomed the discovery that they had a sense of humor.

Roman Catholic cardinals, dressed in red robes and carrying precious miters, marched in a procession with idols. For a token, they changed and played ice hockey against a group of Orthodox priests, chasing an invisible puck with their pastoral staff. Groups of nuns in miniskirts waved pom-poms, cheering them on.

For another token, Muslim mullahs rose from their prayer rugs to kiss Syrian children and provide them with plastic keys to the restroom. Now the children seem to be frightened.

Televangelists, pointing their fingers at me and warning about hell, engaged in group sex for a couple of tokens, and temple prostitutes joined their orgy.

We used up the last of our tokens and couldn't see what some of the other displays would do.

We noticed a platform where a choir of angels were singing hymns of glory and praise.

"They're mannequins!" I announced my great discovery.

They were made out of a substance I could touch. Their wings were paper mâché, which was torn in many places, exposing wire skeletons. I could see that someone had attempted to repair the wings and that the paper was old and yellowing. Above their heads, they had wire rings wrapped in aluminum foil. The rugs that covered them, once white, were held in place with many safety pins. The conductor, dressed in a black jacket and top hat, was waving his hands in mechanical motions. As I came closer, I saw that their voices were not synchronized with the music, which came from a small tape player behind the stage. They looked like a chorus of fish, moving their mouths without voices coming out.

We headed back to the bronze door and knocked on it.

"Who's there?" asked a voice from a Universal speaker. A Universal camera scanned us, and our images appeared somewhere on a Universal monitor, watched by a guardian angel.

The door opened before I could answer, and we entered a small room with bare walls and a single bench.

"Dress! Put on the garments provided."

I saw two transparent plastic overcoats.

"Cover your heads to shield them from the universal glory."

There were caps and surgical masks for us to wear—to protect the universal spirit from the contamination of our breath. I gently placed the cap over the diddle bobbers that were still on my head.

"Wrap your shoes, for you stand on holy ground."

And when we were wrapped up in plastic, like a pair of condoms, the door to the Other Place opened for us.

CHAPTER 16

Millions of insects swarmed around us. I was shocked, astounded by the terrible noise and sight of the insects.

We were in a large abandoned picnic area. Decaying garbage was spreading foul odors, and the insects were feeding on the rubbish. Everything was covered with a gray blanket of living matter.

Whatever I expected the place to be, it wasn't that. This wasn't a place to counter the horrors of the cave. It wasn't the bright side of the gods. It wasn't even for humans.

"Why did you think this would be a place for humans?" asked Peggy. "It's a paradise for insects."

"I'd like to visit a human paradise."

"There isn't one. It was supposed to be nature, but humans arrogantly corrupted the world that was given to them. You must admit that for the flies, this is the ideal place. This is heaven."

"Super flies," I said with sarcasm.

"No need for them to be super," Peggy responded humorlessly. "No need for them to absorb energy through their skin. Here, they can eat and drink and enjoy pleasures. The human concept of paradise is the same. The air isn't polluted, the food isn't poisoned, and the rain isn't acid."

It was a surreal landscape. Clocks were hanging from the trees, spread out on the picnic tables, and laying on the ground like rugs. Many more were probably buried under the masses of insects. The trees were dead, eaten away by the gray masses that covered them, and they now pierced the gray ceiling with their lifeless branches.

Two people were there: a man and a woman were sitting at a table and drinking wine. The middle-aged man wore a black suit and top hat, and he looked familiar. The woman was also middle-aged. Her clothes were dirty and shabby and torn in many places. She looked like someone who had given up on herself.

"Hello," I said. They didn't answer. "May we join you?" I didn't know why I asked. There was a prolonged, uncomfortable silence. They were drinking their wine. I repeated my question, this time louder, trying to be heard over the noise of the insects.

"Oh, dear! Sit down if you must. You need not shout. It's not polite," said the man. They didn't offer us any wine, which was alright with me. I didn't want to drink from their insect-infested glasses anyway.

"Let's go," I whispered to Peggy.

"If you have something to say, speak up. It's not polite to whisper." The man was keen on manners.

"I said that we must go."

"If you must go, why did you come?"

"We are only passing through."

"That doesn't answer my question," said the man.

"I know you. You're Mars," I said to him. "We've met before." And if he was here, Venus must be here, too.

"Mars? No." The man looked puzzled. "Maybe you bought one of my hats. I don't seem to remember you, but that was long ago. No one buys hats anymore. I haven't left this place since I closed the store. And before that, I seldom left."

Despite his denial, his look was piercing, like the look of the gods.

"Where is it that you want to go?" he asked.

"Anywhere that is away from here."

"And where is that?"

"Outside, perhaps."

"Ha, how do you know you aren't there already? I say you are."

"I'm here no doubt, but here is not where I want to be."

"It is simple then, just wish to be here and you will be as happy as we are."

"But I wish to be elsewhere."

"Where?"

"It doesn't really matter, as long as it's not here."

"That's your problem, you'll never be satisfied because you're not sure where you want to be, and if you don't know where you want to be or go, you'll never be content."

"Pay no attention to him," said the woman. "He thinks of himself as the world's greatest philosopher."

"My foot," complained the man.

"Arthritis," said the woman, "It comes from always being on the run. It's all in your mind."

"Next you'll say I'm mad."

"You must admit that there is a method in the madness."

"Yes, it is quite philosophical," said the man. "But who's to say who is mad or not, everything is relative."

"What's your name?" asked the woman, who I was beginning to think looked like Venus.

"Noah Miller."

"This is a great place if you are a fly," the woman said, but her lips didn't move. Then, her lips moved as she said, "he's a ventriloquist. He can speak from anyone he wants to, even from objects. You can tell that it is him by watching their lips. If they don't move, it's him speaking. When you hear objects talk, you can be certain.

"As a child he was small and skinny. The other children made fun of him and he had no friends. He was lonely, no one would speak to him, and he hardly went out. Then he discovered ventriloquism. He practiced talking in the mirror and talked with the objects in his room. He no longer felt lonely. He could lead entire conversations without anyone suspecting it was him. Pretty soon, everyone spoke his words. He had fun making people believe they heard voices talking to them. He could even make them hear voices in the air or from a bush or cloud. Some people thought they were going crazy, others thought it was the voice of a god talking to them."

"That is what I call getting your word across," I said.

"But then it all got into his head, and he thought himself the world's wisest god."

"God?" Maybe he was Mars after all.

"What a heavenly place to be," the woman said, but her lips didn't move.

"It isn't," I said, moving my lips.

"For the insects," said the woman.

"I'm not an insect," I replied.

The man was a true master of his art. Words were coming at me from every direction. They even came even from the insects and dead trees. To make the effect more complete, they were all talking in different voices and occasionally interfering with one another.

". . . place of our bliss . . ."

". . . tranquility . . . nirvana . . ."

". . . holy spirit . . . holy computer . . ."

". . . one with the world . . . we are the world . . ."

"All that is in heaven is for the insects," said the woman.

"Why the insects?"

The answer didn't come from her but seemed to come from all around me.

". . . perfect beings . . ."

". . . perfect life everlasting . . ."

". . . living in harmony with the world . . ."

However, it was the man who provided the final answer. He stood on the table, and instead of a direct answer, he recited a poem:

A spider webs his net

Without learning he can.

Man who learns

Webbing, he cannot.

"Bravo, bravo," the woman applauded. I joined her applause, and the man bowed like an actor on stage.

"I wrote it myself," he said. "The more you know, the less you understand. And what you know, you can't tell. Words obscure it. Only humans think words are important. And where do they store their words?" The man pointed behind him toward a platform with a computer console. "That is where the words are stored."

This small platform was the only place without any insects. Someone was sitting on a black chair next to the computer, but I couldn't see who it was because his back was turned. Magnetic tapes were rotating in the computer cabinets beside the platform.

I walked closer to the platform to find out more about him and the computer. This could be the master computer that controls this place, or a computer that made the gods' assignments in the academy and kept their records. What a great discovery. It may hold all the answers.

Before I could get any closer a swarm of killer bees came and blocked my way, and then there was a sudden silence. The buzzing stopped. The flies and all the other flying insects landed on the ground. Just a moment ago they were buzzing, and the air was thick with anticipation. The insects' eyes began to glow. The computer reels rotated faster, and I saw a surge of radiation coming from it.

"The word, listen to the word."

Were my diddle bobbers useful now? Was I about to hear the universal message?

I heard nothing.

The killer bees landed on the ground and left the platform unguarded. I was able to get close enough to read the computer screen: "Enter your security code." I saw an invisible hand insert a universal decoder into a slot, and invisible fingers typed in the code. A state of euphoria spread around.

But I still didn't hear anything.

"Only the insects can hear," said the Peggy.

I took off my diddle bobbers and threw them to the ground. I was convinced they were useless.

"Tell them about the word," said the woman.

"The word," said the man, talking slowly, emphasizing every syllable, "existed prior to the beginning and is contained in the number seven."

"Seven?" I was amazed by the stupidity of it.

"Seven?" Peggy echoed my question, but I detected a hint of mockery in her tone.

"What a letdown," I said. "All this is truly ridiculous."

"No one believes it. It is just too simple for people to accept."

"Can you prove it?" I asked. Peggy nodded her head in agreement. This was a grave mistake. The man pulled out a pocket calculator and faced the insects and humans.

"These are events that will take place when humankind succumbs to oblivion. A time will come in human history when they will become so dependent upon computers and other electronic devices that they will lose the capability of independent thinking. The microchips will rule. Robots will perform most physical tasks, and computers will perform all mental functions. One plant will need to produce silicon chips for the entire world. Then, either through negligence or oversight, a beetle will penetrate into the central memory of the silicon production unit and chew the part of the chip where the number seven is stored.

"At first it will go unnoticed, but gradually all chips will be replaced by the defective ones—those without the number seven, without the word. Everything will begin to fall apart. New cars won't run, planes will collide in midair, and bridges will collapse. Every imaginable catastrophic event will happen. Nuclear plants will melt down and poisonous gasses will escape and kill thousands. All scientific theories will be rejected because the data will no longer support them."

"Why can't they simply replace the faulty chip?"

"Good question. They will become so dependent upon the computers and the chips that they will no longer be able to check the accuracy of anything independently."

"But seven is a symbol and could be replaced."

"Yes, it could. But it is not just the symbol that will go missing but also the concept of seven. Without it, nothing else can be true, not even the value of Pi. Humankind had the benefit of the word for a long time, that is, until all this happened."

I found myself drawn into his absurd fantasy with ridiculous arguments of my own.

"The bug could have chewed away a different portion of the chip, let's say number eight. What then?" I asked

"Nothing. The word is a prime number."

"Three?"

"The same result as with seven."

"So, seven is not the word!" I said with glee.

"The word is whatever destroys harmony.

"But . . ."

"No buts. Every word is the word if it is missing. Its absence damages the harmony of the world. Like a black hole that gradually pulls everything into it. No matter how small it is at the beginning, everything falls in eventually, and after that humankind will no longer exist."

"Nonsense!"

For a while, no one spoke, not even the insects. I poured some wine into a Styrofoam cup, but I had no intention of drinking it.

"I still can't see how a single missing number will cause the demise of humankind," Peggy said, breaking the silence.

"It's the robots. Soon, they will perform all physical tasks. Millions will lose their jobs. There will be a growing number of products that people will no longer be able to afford. This will result in a worldwide economic depression, and the crisis will continue until the robots reach a solution: They begin producing self-destructing products, whose sole purpose is to destroy other products and to destroy themselves in the process. Humankind will be destroyed along with them."

"What a preposterous idea," said Peggy. But it made sense to me now. All current weapon systems were like the defective products of the robots who had lost the word.

A bell began ringing, and red lights flashed and danced around the platform with the computer. A word was spreading among the insects, and they erected their antennas. The air was heavy, loaded with the weight of the message. There was more excitement than before, but we, the humans, didn't share it with them. The entire atmosphere was building up toward a climax.

Crickets began rubbing their legs and making mating sounds, insects were dancing and courting, aphrodisiac odors spread as Spanish flies embraced each other and squeezed out their essences, and bugs were blushing in many colors. There was a sexual excitement in the air. A bell gave a signal, and then the insects mounted each other to mate.

Due to a lack of room, or for sheer pleasure, they mated with whatever kind of insect was next to them. Ants mated with bed bugs, praying mantis with roaches, and other combinations. They mated in pairs, in groups, and on their own. It was a pure primordial sexual energy—uninhibited, existing for its own sake.

When they all came together, the entire place was charged with energy, like being inside a bolt of lightning. The energy entered into us and charged us with the irresistible universal power. Peggy and I hugged and kissed passionately, and then undressed each other.

"Maybe we shouldn't."

"Why not? This is heaven, isn't it?"

"It doesn't seem right."

"I've wanted to do it for a long time."

"Oh . . . yes."

I united with Peggy and with the universal energy field. She didn't feel artificial, and her organs felt like they were real. Even her skin was smooth and soft.

"Pam," I cried out when I came.

The insects formed a circle around us and watched. When we separated from each other, they applauded and clapped their wings.

"How embarrassing," Peggy said.

The platform turned dark again. There was a single beam of light shining on something. I saw the true Holy Grail standing on the computer monitor. It was a Styrofoam cup.

CHAPTER 17

After we had rested for a while we put on our clothes and left the Other Place. Peggy lead me to a metal staircase that led upward. From the bottom, I couldn't see the top.

"All you have to do is climb the stairs to the exit," Peggy told me.

"Aren't you coming with me?"

"I'm sorry, but I must stay. I have work to catch up on."

I didn't try to persuade her otherwise. She belonged to the cave now and not the outside.

"I love my work, and besides," she said in an unconvincing tone, "this is a great place to meet people. Everyone comes here sooner or later. Be sure to come back, there is so much more to see."

I knew I would never come back by choice.

My footsteps created hollow sounds on the metal stairs, the sound of approaching the exit. I climbed until I stopped counting my steps. The stairs continued to spiral upward without mercy. The bottom of the cave was getting farther away, but the exit didn't seem any closer. And although there were many stairs, and no landings to rest on, I didn't feel tired or out of breath. I could go on climbing forever. Was it another of the gods' tricks? A carrot dangling in front of a mule—as much as one tries to reach the exit, the distance remains unchanged. I began climbing faster, and the more steps I climbed, the more of them there seemed to be. I felt despair. This could be my assignment in the cave: to keep climbing upward without end and without getting tired, perpetually hoping to reach an exit at the top. The staircase was engulfed in darkness, except for a dim light illuminating the steps ahead of me. It was like my dream of the endless plain, only this was real.

I was determined to keep climbing and be free of this terrible place; free to return to the institution and to resume my life as it was before the time capsule and before I was involved with the Holy Grail. Thoughts about Pam and life as it used to be made the climb tolerable.

I could almost touch the darkness around me. It was thick and heavy. I was thinking about being home with Pam when suddenly the stairs ended and I reached a landing. There was a small door with an exit sign on it. I inhaled. Freedom.

***

I blinked and found myself standing in front of the institution. I walked inside, intending to demand a formal discharge so I could resume the regular course of my life. I would get this, even at the price of the dreadful shock therapy treatment. I walked up to the receptionist, but she didn't recognize me.

"Hello, may I help you?" she asked.

"I'm Noah Miller."

"Who are you here to see?"

"Dr. Green, I guess."

"The outpatient department is on the other side of the building."

"I'm a patient. I came for my discharge." When she heard this she pressed a hidden button to summon two attendants in white overalls, and they escorted me to Dr. Green's office.

"I'm glad you're back," said Dr. Green, looking rather pleased with himself.

"I bet you are. I came to get my discharge."

"Where were you trying to go? We were worried about you!"

"You wouldn't believe me."

"Try me."

"I was in hell."

"Ha, ha, ha." I expected nothing different from him, but I had nothing to lose anyway.

"I was also in heaven."

"Ha, ha, ha."

"Well, I told you that you wouldn't believe me."

"Heaven and hell are within each one of us," he said, dismissing the matter with a philosophical cliché, but then he asked me to describe them to him.

"Heaven is not for humans, it is for the insects."

"Interesting," was his only reply, I felt free to give him all the details.

"The insects enjoy everything humans envision to be there: good food, listening to the universal secrets coming from the universal computer, and good sex. And hearing the word."

"And what is the word?"

"Seven."

"Seven?" I knew he would find it ridiculous.

"Yes." I knew that I shouldn't mention it to him, but it made no difference, he had already made up his mind about my best course of treatment. He didn't ask about the Holy Grail, nor about the other part of my visit—about hell.

I decided never to tell any of this to Pam, she might think I was completely out of my mind. Our meeting a few hours later was all kisses and hugs and lots of tears. It was brief, in order not to upset me too much before the next crucial step of my recovery.

"See you at home soon, darling."

"I'll be waiting, darling."

Even Nancy no longer opposed me receiving the shock therapy.

"You will be out in no time, next week possibly," she told me.

"I've heard such promises before."

"The treatment works wonders. You really will feel nothing. We are simply trying to help you."

Pam had signed the consent papers some time ago. They had convinced her to do so with misleading information about my condition undoubtedly, fabricated data about the success of the treatment.

"You have a nine out of ten chance of the treatment working," said Nancy.

"What if I don't respond positively?"

"At the worst, you will be as you are."

"What a comfort. I prefer to remain the same without the treatment." But, as I expected, they paid no attention to my concerns. My fears simply didn't count. They were armed with theories, their shaky statistical results, and with legal definitions of my condition and their responsibilities. The truth carried no weight.

I was scared. I felt like I was back in the cave, a place none of them believed existed. I was helpless. It was completely within their power to determine what was good for me. Dr. Green just loved this. Even Nancy agreed with him, although she had stood between me and the dreadful treatment at one time.

I was no longer a person, not even a patient: I was nothing but a subject. And that made the whole difference. A person reacts with emotions and with a spectrum of other responses. A subject only responds in one of two ways, positively or negatively. I hated them for what they were about to do to me, and for deceiving Pam about it.

"The abnormal hallucinations should completely disappear and you will resume a normal life. There is nothing to be afraid of," Nancy assured me. "I'll be right there beside you the whole time." But I really didn't care. I didn't consider her a friend any longer.

Carol, the new nurse, came to give me a shot in the morning. I shouldn't have accepted the tokens for the tenth level of pain. I should have left them there in the receptacle. It was part of the torment, pain delayed; I was given the illusion of escaping from it. If I hadn't taken the payment, maybe I would have been spared.

They strapped me to a table, like a sacrifice on an altar, but no ram was waiting in the bushes to take my place. They shaved part of my hair and spread a cold conductive ointment on the bald spots. The electrodes against my temples were cold. I closed my eyes. The last thing I saw was Dr. Green smiling.

Then, blacklight engulfed me, and for the last time, I saw magnificent things— wonderful colors and dancing lights, all creating enchanting patterns. I was in the dark and felt secure. Then I began spinning around, slowly at first and then faster and faster. There was a large tree there, and I spun around it. There were other objects also spinning with me and creating a giant whirlpool. I knew the tree, it was the tree from hill 537, the secret base of the Space Warriors. The tree was a black hole into which all objects were falling. The more matter fell inside, the darker it became. And the darkness spread around until all the light of the world fell inside of it. And as more matter fell in, the deeper the hold became. It was getting deeper and deeper, until only I remained outside. Then I fell in.

I saw a dancer motioning me to join him, and we danced together, circling around, spinning together. I saw that I was dancing with my mother. She was beautiful, like in her pictures. The objects dancing around us disintegrated into a soup of molecules, then reassembled again into new objects. They were wonderful objects that I had never seen before. I was euphoric. I was one with my mother and with them.

Suddenly it all disappeared, and I was alone in the darkness. I called out for my mother, but she didn't answer. I called out the name of Shiva, the prince of dancers, but he didn't answer either. I wanted to ask him if he was the director of the academy.

Then I was spinning again, and I called out for Pam. Someone was holding my hand. I opened my eyes and saw her beside me. Only then did I realize that there was no pain. I extended my hand to grab hers, but it closed on empty space, like a hologram or an illusion.

When I opened my eyes again the spinning had stopped, and I saw Pam smiling.

I was cured.

***

Red is red again, and blue is blue. All colors have names that other people understand. I don't see the other colors anymore, but I know they are still there.

I'm waiting in my room. Pam is taking care of some formalities in the office. I take a small bottle of Bubble Bee Soap Bubble solution out of my pocket and blow some bubbles through the plastic wand attached to the cap. They are all perfectly shaped, reflecting all the colors in the room but having no color of their own.

When I leave my room to go home, a Styrofoam cup is resting on top of the television. It has the number seven scratched on it.

258

ABOUT THE AUTHORS

Yair Riback was a psychologist as well as an award-winning artist and passionate writer. Yair received his undergraduate degree from the Hebrew University in Jerusalem where he majored in Mathematics and Physics. After earning his M.A. and Ph.D. in Psychology from the University of Pittsburgh, Yair returned to his birthplace of Israel where he worked for the Israeli Army conducting psychological research. In 1971, Yair and Nira relocated to Louisville, KY where he continued his psychological research and work, this time for a private company doing research for the U.S. Army at Fort Knox. Years later, he switched positions and went to work for the Kentucky Legislative Research Commission in Frankfort, Kentucky. Yair also worked with Nira at their private psychotherapy practice, and as a team, they utilized a variety of therapeutic modalities to assist their patients. Inspired by Nira, Yair eventually retired and dedicated himself to his artistic pursuits such as writing, painting, and photography.

Nira graduated from Kibbutzim College of Education and Technology in Tel-Aviv and continued her studies in Jewish History, Biblical Studies and Hebrew Literature at a branch of the Hebrew University in Tel-Aviv. She worked as a teacher for fourteen years, including three years where she served as an exchange teacher in Pittsburgh as part of a program by the Israeli Ministry of Education. In Pittsburgh she taught Hebrew, History and Geography of Israel. After completing three years as an exchange teacher in the United States, Nira returned to Israel for two years, and then permanently relocated to the United States with her husband, Yair, and their two daughters. They eventually settled in Louisville, Kentucky. Nira went back to school at the University of Louisville where she earned a Master's Degree in Expressive Psychotherapy. She was one of the first expressive psychotherapist to open a private practice, and she continued her work there for twenty-five years. Now that she's retired, Nira enjoys traveling, reading, writing, painting, and spending time with her two daughters, five grandchildren and great grandson.

REVIEWS

I read straight through and didn't want to put it down. It's a real page turner. The narrator is great and the plot (erratic as it is) moves forward, really tumbles forward at breakneck speed. It definitely pulled me in and at times gave me the weird feeling of not being quite sure if it was delusion or reality.
(P. Smith)

Yair Riback launches readers directly into the uncanny from the moment that Noah's story begins with his pointed observations. The novel functions similarly to his experience trying to find Mr. Brown's office in Omega Corporation's headquarters in the first chapter: all doors are unmarked and the journey from point A to point B is met with twists and turns that keep you on your toes. He senses the energy of certain objects, such as a replica of the Holy Grail, which pushes him against the status quo in search of the truth that he feels is hiding everywhere, including in his new position in the company. But, as Noah teaches us, the truth carries no weight based on how everyone else perceives it; our destiny remains out of our earthly control and in the hands of the gods.
(C. McKee)

Reality and fantasy collide in this thrilling novel by Yair Riback. When the right side of Noah Miller's brain takes over, he sees the world as no one else does. His visions and adventures are jarring, compelling, and extraordinary. In this thought-provoking, philosophical novel, Riback explores the intricacies of human nature, following in the footsteps of experimental, postmodernist writers like Don DeLillo and Kurt Vonnegut. A must-read for those who are enraptured by hyperreality and magical realism.
(V. Shircliffe)

I spent a long time while reading and even after reading trying to figure out if Noah's visions were real, but ultimately, it did not matter either way. (I think they were real, if that matters at all.) We are put into his perspective, and if we do not believe him, it means that we are more like Dr. Green, Pam, and later, Nancy, who all do not listen and can't *imagine* like Noah does.

I think the novel is most successful in small, brief moments and asides that do things like acknowledge the past, give Noah more character, or give wry commentary on the world.

(I. Aigbedion)